NIGHTFALL

Brilliant young astronomer Professor Charles Brown is in possession of dangerous information. Bound by the Official Secrets Act, yet driven by an inner compulsion to tell the truth, he wrestles with his conscience.

To tell the world would unleash untold panic. But to give no warning . . . ?

Nightfall is the spine-chilling sequel to Christopher Bryan's first thriller, *Night of the Wolf*.

For my mother

NIGHTFALL

CHRISTOPHER BRYAN

A LION PAPERBACK
Tring · Belleville · Sydney

Published by
Lion Publishing plc
Icknield Way, Tring, Herts, England
ISBN 0 7459 1003 3
Albatross Books Pty Ltd
PO Box 320, Sutherland, NSW 2232, Australia
ISBN 0 86760 669 X

First edition 1986

British Library Cataloguing in Publication Data

Bryan, Christopher
Nightfall.
I. Title
823′.914[F] PR6052.R8/
0 7459 1003 3

The characters and situations in this book are entirely imaginary and bear no relation to any real person or actual happening.

Printed and bound in Great Britain by
Cox and Wyman, Reading

CONTENTS

AUTHOR'S NOTE

I ought to acknowledge that the idea for making a story out of a galactic explosion comes from John Gribbin's book *White Holes*, where he actually says that it would make a good theme for a novel. The idea is also used (as Gribbin points out) in Fred and Geoffrey Hoyle's exciting book *Inferno*. Of course, none of these is in any way responsible for the use I have made of the theme.

I should like to thank Phyllis Davies for kindly allowing me to print her poem 'White Dog: Splodger' ar the beginning of the book; and Sue Armentrout for many helpful suggestions.

WHITE DOG: SPLODGER

It seems she is always there, a white wraith
under the classic oak.
Relaxed but dignified she lies, taking the slope
of the long field in her dark eyes, idly gazing
at people who pass with children, intently watching
other dogs who might invade or desecrate her domain.

There is mystique about her, a hint of but half-
remembered ancestors who bayed the Northern Lights.
Perhaps she still hears the rustle of the ageless
forest, inhales the timeless scents that constitute
her world.

Of what does she dream through those inscrutable
deep eyes, how much is forgotten of her pre-domesticity?
She lies curled, her whole attitude one of content,
ears pricked or flattened according to her mood or
instinct.

We love but do not possess her. We are privileged to
share happiness we have tried to create.
Under the dapple of sunlight she lies, at eventide still
we see her, when Autumn casts lengthening shadows.

In moonlight she becomes indistinct, whiter than the
thrown beam, before the snow comes she will have gone.
The oak will be leafless and bare-branched.

But I shall always see her in her favourite place,
thick-coated, warm and friendly, eager in response,
dignified and full of repose . . .

So stay beneath the oak that marks your guarding place,
When I pass I shall not disturb . . .

PHYLLIS DAVIES

Chapter One

Beginnings

Explosion.
A pebble dropped at the galaxy's centre.
Ripples spreading.
Thirty thousand light years distant from earth.
But approaching.
Through suns. Systems. Planets.
Approaching.
Through the millenia.
Approaching.
Plato. The Buddha. Moses.
Jesus the Christ.
Mahomet.
Approaching.
Through times of love and times of hate.
Athens and Jerusalem.
Rome and Constantinople.
Approaching.
London. Adelaide. Ontario.
Washington. Bonn.
Approaching.

The Venerable Michael Aarons, Archdeacon of East London and Rector of St Andrew's, Holborn Circus, gathered his papers together, put them into a document case, and looked at his watch.

12.20 p.m. Good. His sermon was ready, and the taxi should arrive at any minute. He relaxed, and permitted himself a moment of pleasant anticipation. He would not normally have been pleased by the prospect of a journey across London to Paddington Station, followed by commitment to the vagaries of British Rail – but on this occasion there were compensations. He was going to Exeter, where he had accepted an invitation to preach at the smaller (and older) of the two University chapels. To tell the truth, long friendship with one of the professors of education, rather than any direct connection with the University, was what had led to this; and whilst preaching at St Luke's Chapel offered justification for a rare Sunday away from London, it was hardly the chief cause of his pleasure. What he did look forward to, as he had admitted to himself earlier that morning while packing his case, was a weekend of good conversation and renewed acquaintance with his friend. No doubt, he conceded wryly, this was not particularly apostolic of him, but the facts could not be denied.

Slowly, he began to tidy the remaining papers on his desk. Leaflets on Diocesan policy (which he supposed he would have to read at some time or other) went into a boxfile. Käsemann's *An Die Römer* and Davies' *Paul and Rabbinic Judaism* he put back into a bookcase. Then, there was this morning's *Times*. He stopped, and frowned.

A fly in the ointment.

Not, of course, *The Times* itself (though it was not as good as it used to be, and sometimes he thought of changing to *The Guardian)*. No. What troubled him was the content of one of its articles – something that sounded to him like very bad news indeed. Pursing his lips, he took out his keys, unlocked a drawer in the desk, and withdrew from it a manilla folder marked in red with the three letters 'A. P. S.' He took from the newspaper a page, tore from the page the article, and placed that in the folder. Then he replaced the folder, and re-locked the drawer.

In a pleasant house in the city of Salisbury, about eighty miles south-west of London, Splodger the dog jumped to her feet, gave a short, joyful yelp, and trotted downstairs. Pooh the cat flicked her tail, and deigned to look out of the window. A few seconds later, and even the merely human ears of Chief Inspector David Adam could hear the mutter and swish of the approaching car.

He put down his coffee and the paper, got to his feet, and walked across the room.

He was nervous.

The car door slammed. Footsteps on the path. Key in the lock. The opening front door, rattling as it always did. Then the sound of Splodger bouncing, and Elizabeth's voice fending off the welcome. 'Yes! Yes! I know! All right! Good girl! Hello! I'm back.'

They met half-way, on the stairs.

She grinned at him, and her eyes twinkled.

'Well?' he said.

But he knew the answer before he asked.

'*Yes!*' she replied. 'I am. It's positive.'

'Well!' It was a feeble remark, but he felt feeble. Shy. Almost as if they were on a first date. All he could do was look in her eyes and grin. Then, gently, he took her in his arms and kissed her.

'So,' she said at last, 'I duly announce that, barring accidents, Sproglet Adam is preparing to be launched upon the world.'

'Fabulous!' He shook his head. There was a pause, then – 'Sproglet's a good name,' he said.

'Yes,' she said. 'I thought so.'

Another pause.

'What about a cup of coffee, then?'

'All right then. But darling – ' she giggled.

'Yes?'

'I suppose you know you sound just like the Nescafé

commercial?'

'Good Lord,' he said. 'Perhaps I do.'

They started to walk down the stairs.

'Of course,' he said, 'we're going to have a terrible job explaining all this to Splodger.'

'Well, Splodger was here first,' she said. 'If Sproglet and Splodger don't get on, I'm afraid Sproglet will just have to go.'

'Yes,' he said. 'Well. I suppose that's reasonable enough. No one could object to that.'

Hand in hand, they wandered towards the kitchen.

Michael Aarons had locked the manilla folder away, but his thoughts continued to dwell on it.

'A. P. S.' The Academy for Philosophical Studies.

To Aarons, a sinister title – and with good reason.

Suffice it to say* that for years Michael Aarons and several colleagues – priests, doctors, and others in the caring professions – had found themselves counselling numbers of mentally disturbed persons who turned out, in one way or another, to be victims of the Academy's activities. Aarons and his colleagues also found that the Academy was skilled in covering its tracks; it retained excellent lawyers, and never created situations where it could have been held responsible at law. Then, during the previous October, Aarons' friend Chief Inspector David Adam had become involved. In the course of what at first seemed to be a routine police enquiry, David found evidence linking the Academy to a trail, some twenty years long, of disappearances and death. As always, the evidence was not sufficient to sustain charges in court, but it was considerably more than David was willing to ignore. He persisted in his questions, crossing paths in the process with one of the Academy's governors – a man named James Darrell.

* Those interested in the full story will find it in *Night of the Wolf*

Then came the night of October the thirty-first – All Hallows' Eve. Almost by accident (though Aarons was inclined to say, by Providence) David interrupted the Academy's governors as they were performing a ceremony: *Beriyt et-Mavet*, the Covenant with Death, a ritual whose ill intention and real effectiveness Aarons had little reason to doubt. At this point David himself (though he and Michael Aarons had been over the matter several times) found it hard to describe or understand precisely what happened. He had found himself accompanied by a mysterious she-wolf, who attacked the governors and halted the rite. There was a fire. Several of the governors died. One at least – Darrell – escaped. Angered by David's questions, it seemed he had vowed to offer David's wife through the ceremony to the dark power it invoked. But with the ceremony broken, Darrell had driven through the night to Salisbury, and attempted to murder Elizabeth. Only in the nick of time, Michael Aarons and David arrived to stop him. The wretched Darrell was arrested, but then, in custody, killed himself – believing, so Aarons suspected, that since he had failed to obtain the life he vowed, his own life was forfeit.

So matters had stood on All Saints' Day of the previous year. Aarons was not likely to forget the date.

Now there was the article in this morning's *Times*, suggesting to the priest that after only a few months the Academy's plans were again maturing. He wondered if David had seen it? Should he get in touch with him? In some ways he hesitated to disturb his friends by dragging up the matter again. And yet, he felt some responsibility, too. Perhaps then, he should phone?

There was a ring at the front door bell.

The taxi.

Abruptly, Michael Aarons started from his thoughts. Well, there was nothing he could do about it for the moment. On Monday, he must give the matter his attention, and make a decision. For now, the main task was to get himself to Paddington Station. He put the rest of *The Times* into the waste-paper basket, picked up his document case, said goodbye to the cats (Mrs Owens, his housekeeper, would see to them over the weekend), and left the study. He had already put his suitcase in the hall.

What Michael Aarons did not know – what, in the nature of things, he could not have known – was that a series of events was already in train that would overtake both his present information and his decisions. These events had begun, indeed, several months earlier, with an observation by a group of scientists on the other side of the world.

Chapter Two

The Astronomers

Siding Spring Observatory, New South Wales. Several months earlier.

Charlie Brown scraped the hair out of his eyes, pushed his glasses up on his nose, and again bent his lanky figure over the photographic plate. The others crowded round him. Earnest faces, eager and puzzled. Here and there, a hint of tension.

'It's a bigger mess than the others,' observed John Daniels cheerfully. His broad Australian vowels contrasted sharply with the crisp tones of Shirley Lucas, one of the British group.

'It's clear enough for what we need,' she said.

Charlie pursed his lips, frowned again at the plate, and finally straightened up. He seemed to have made a decision.

'Yes,' he said. 'It is. What do you think we've got?'

She hesitated, then – 'A supernova, I suppose.'

'At the centre of the galaxy. Sagittarius A. Does that say anything to you?'

'It's got to be somewhere. Why not there?' said Daniels.

'OK,' said Charlie. 'Point taken. Where would *you* start?'

There was a pause.

Finally Daniels gestured at the figures on the whiteboard. 'Well, there's the redshift. Pretty extreme. Which suggests it's moving away from us. I guess I agree with Shirl. I think we're looking at a supernova, way beyond our galaxy.'

'And its appearing centre is just coincidence?' said Charlie.

'I guess so.'

Another pause. Someone lit a cigarette. Then –

'Maybe the redshift doesn't mean distancing,' said Shirley. 'It doesn't have to.'

'Agreed,' said Charlie. 'And in that case?'

'In that case – ' she hesitated, considering the direction of her own logic. 'In that case there might *not* be movement away.'

'Yes?' said Charlie.

'It might even be moving towards us.'

'Strikes!' said Daniels, abruptly seeing the point. 'The Seyfert effect.'

'Yes,' she nodded. 'Only this time, of course, it would be us.'

'Exactly,' said Charlie Brown. 'Ladies and gentlemen, I think the nucleus of our galaxy has exploded.'

Needless to say, Charlie Brown was not sure. During the next few hours the Anglo-Australian team consulted. With the Americans at Cerro Tololo. With the Europeans at La Silla. Someone has said that cosmology is like religion – a large amount of belief and a rather small amount of information – but in this case, the sense of certainty grew. Each new dialogue confirmed either the calculations, or the observations, or both. Step by step, minute by minute, and Charlie's first wild insight seemed increasingly like the necessary hypothesis. Finally, he took steps to inform the British and Australian governments, told the telephonist that even if the world ended in the next few hours he was not to be disturbed, and went to bed.

There, he had the Dream.

As ever, it left him confused and fearful, save that now old fears mingled with fresh anxieties to create new discords, and even, at some remote depth, possibilities of harmony.

The Dream had been a recurring feature of his childhood.

Until about the age of ten, it occurred once every six or seven months. In puberty and adolescence, its frequency declined. It came once in a year. Then after two years. Then five. Then there must have been tweleve or fifteen years during which he almost forgot it. Now, it came again. He was in a lofty hall that gleamed with cream and gold. There were handsome pillars and a high ceiling. He stood on a huge chess board. Across shining squares of black and white came a man wearing a long black robe. 'You must!' said the man. 'You must!' Then, as always, Charlie awoke, perspiring and afraid. In childhood he had cried for his mother. There had been kisses and warmth and Jack the dog and Peter the cat to restore the world to sanity. Later, in adolescent pride, he refused to confess his dread, but switched on the bedside light and left it on until, after fitful sleep, he woke again to find it shining in the morning light.

Now he got up, went to the window and looked out at the New South Wales landscape. He stood for a while, then remembered there was a machine down the hall that served chocolate. Maybe that, and an aspirin, would help him sleep. Tonight looked like being busy again.

Sir George Havers, Secretary of State to the Cabinet, was worried. He pushed back greying hair with his right hand, and turned the pages of the report with his left. Then he nodded.

'Yes, Charles, I admit it. It looks serious. Though of course it's too soon to be sure.'

Sir Charles Dancy, Permanent Under-Secretary for the Department of the Environment, looked at the Cabinet Secretary quizzically, but said nothing.

'Meanwhile,' continued Sir George, 'obviously, all this is absolutely under wraps. Can't have panic on the streets and all that.'

'No,' said Sir Charles. 'Exactly.'

'The PM's seeing me at ten,' continued the other. 'The Australians already know. Washington and the Europeans will have been advised by their own teams. My guess is they'll consult at once, then take it straight to the United Nations.'

'Yes,' said Sir Charles. 'That would seem logical.'

'What we need, however, is a UK scenario. Probable effects. Survival zones. That sort of thing. Then – *solvitur ambulando*. Can you get someone onto that?'

'I have done,' said Sir Charles. 'Discreetly. You should have something – a first draft at any rate – for your meeting.'

'Splendid,' said Sir George.

'I'm afraid it doesn't look good.'

'No.'

Sir George closed the report, got up from his desk, walked slowly over to the tall window, and looked down. Buses. Taxis. People. Whitehall in the rain. The sound of traffic came only faintly through double glazing. The room itself was quiet, dominated by the rich tick of an ormolu clock.

Abruptly, he turned back to his colleague.

'Of course,' he said, 'it may turn out to be a fuss about nothing.'

'Yes,' said Sir Charles, who had more scientific training than Sir George, and perhaps appreciated better than he the implications of the report. 'Well, yes, of course. It may turn out to be that.' He met the other's gaze. 'But I shouldn't bank on it, George. I really shouldn't.'

Chapter Three

Many Nations

The multicoloured flags outside the United Nations Headquarters flapped and strained at their halyards, then sank in uneasy calm. A tug hooted mournfully from the East River. The air above New York City was tense, grey and gusty; and perhaps something other than fancy saw that tension reflected in more than one of the representatives who now emerged from oversized and beflagged limousines, preparatory to attending a meeting of the United Nations Scientific and Economic Liaison Committee, scheduled for 3.00 p.m. Charlie Brown emerged among them, self-consciously trying to look as if he were as at home with the situation as his two companions, career diplomats both of them, and veterans to the United Nations.

He started to look at his watch for the fourth time in five minutes, recognized the movement as pure displacement action, and controlled it. The fact was, the whole situation unnerved him. He was by nature neither politician, diplomat, nor civil servant. To his soul he was an academic. Sudden involvement in summonses to the Foreign Office, signings of the Official Secrets Act, no-notice flights to New York on Concorde, and diplomatic receptions were all, to him, quite disorienting.

He had visited New York on other occasions – once, while on holiday, and once for a scientific congress. But this was the first time he had been so close to the United Nations complex. He paused deliberately, craning his neck to take in the thirty-nine storeyed slab of the Secretariat Tower, its side a green-tinted mirror reflecting the dull Manhattan sky.

One of his companions noticed his gaze.

'Mangled Corbusier,' he observed laconically. 'Not exactly great architecture, but certainly a remarkable experience. Come on. We'll be late.'

Slowly, Charlie Brown followed.

The United Nations Scientific and Economic Liaison Committee (UNSELC) is one of the less-publicized sections of that organization created by the world to lead it into the paths of peace. It is, to be precise, a confidential subcommittee of the Economic and Social Council, whose function, according to Article 62 of the Charter, is to make suggestions and submit reports 'with respect to international economic, social, . . . health, and related matters.' To such a subcommittee the Secretary-General may, at his discretion, pass matters of particular delicacy for consideration and non-binding recommendation. And perhaps because the committee's words and acts are less subject to the world's attention than those that pass in the fiercer light of the General Assembly or the Security Council, sometimes the world's business is better forwarded by them. A word may be dropped in passing, a hint that a member of the delegation for the Republic of X has heard it mentioned (unofficially, of course) that his government might be prepared to take a view on such and such an issue that it could not yet dream of countenancing publicly, if by any chance the government of the State of Y were prepared to consider such and such a modification of its own position. By such hints and counter-hints, the world's business goes forward.

On this occasion, UNSELC had its own business, and it had chosen to avoid publicity even more deliberately than usual. The session was to be closed and confidential. The peoples of the world – certainly of the West – have come to expect what journalism euphemistically refers to as 'leaks' – from the White House; from the Cabinet of Her Majesty's Government; from the secret conclaves of Prime Ministers and Presidents. No doubt, in an age dominated by news coverage, 'leaks' have become virtually an instrument of government. 'Informed sources', 'moles', strayed files and stolen tapes, sometimes a source of embarrassment, are yet as often a means of communication by which the waters are tested, public reaction to a new proposal explored, whilst those in office still retain an attitude of detachment, disclaiming all knowledge, if need be. Yet occasionally the world is staggered by some disclosure after the event that reveals just how well the cabinets and councils keep their secrets if they have a mind to. No doubt the world would be staggered more often, were it not that those secrets which the leaders of the nations choose to keep – they choose to keep. One such example was now presented, for those who knew, by UNSELC. Every member government of the United Nations was, at the highest level, aware of the matter that occupied the Committee's attention; yet not one word of the matter, not one inkling or suspicion, not so much as an 'I could if I would', had reached the world's media. In a nutshell – there were no leaks.

Charlie and the other members of the British delegation were early. A brief meeting to confer over papers – to note that there was nothing new to note – and by general agreement they went to their places. Several delegations were already there, including the Americans. Charlie gazed amiably about him, then noted with a sudden surge of interest the blonde head of Jacqueline Austin. Of course! – scientific liaison – she would be with their delegation. What more natural?

He had met her two nights earlier at a reception, bumping up against her in a crowded mêlée of cocktails and conversation.

'What's your name?' he had said – the cocktails making him bolder than usual, for flirtation was not his strong suit.

'Jacquie,' she replied. 'Jacqueline Austin. Austin as in Texas,' she added helpfully.

'And in motor-car,' he observed.

'What?'

'Sorry!' he said. 'An obscure British machine!'

'What's *your* name?' she asked.

'Charlie. Charlie Brown,' – then, not to be outdone – 'as in Peanuts.'

'And Redskins!' she added triumphantly.

'What?' he said.

'Oh dear! Another culture gap! You certainly wouldn't know about our football. Don't worry. Charlie Brown's a hero.'

The truth is, Charlie was so ignorant about sport, he probably wouldn't have known if the man had been a British footballer. Still, it was good to know his namesake stood well in her eyes. Conversation prospered delightfully for several minutes. He learned that she was a consultant psychologist working for the US government at the United Nations. Then came their hosts, dragging them both away to people they 'must' meet. In the crowd, he did not see her again.

Now she was there. Perhaps he could see her after the meeting? Dinner? Would that be a breach of diplomatic etiquette? Or a strengthening of the 'special relationship'?

The Committee assembled quickly and with surprisingly little noise for an assembly so large – though no doubt the acoustics of the superbly-designed chamber had something to do with that. Such murmur as there was stilled rapidly as the group responsible for this afternoon's presentation filed to the platform. The convener rose to her feet. There was silence.

The main presentation was brief. Indeed there was, in one sense, little to say. All knew why they were assembled. On first November an Anglo-Australian team of astronomers using the 150-inch telescope at the Siding Spring Observatory in New South Wales had observed what was at first taken for a supernova. Subsequent observation led to the conclusion that it was in fact an early manifestation (from the Earth's point of view) of an explosion at the nucleus of the Milky Way – our own galaxy. The Anglo-Australian instrument had, as it happened, been trained on that segment of sky for sometime, and so, by a comparison of photographic plates taken throughout the period, the astronomers had been able to mark the appearance of the phenomenon to within twelve hours. Siding Star (so someone had named it, and the name stuck) had appeared between 01.20 and 12.20 UT (GMT) on 1 November. Other observatories had later confirmed both the observations and their interpretation.

The situation appeared to be this. Thirty thousand years ago there had been an explosion at the heart of our galaxy. In the universe as a whole, such explosions are, of course, not uncommon. The centre of the explosion being thirty thousand light years distant from our planetary system, its results were just now beginning to arrive. First (the speed of light vastly exceeding anything else) we should see it: indeed, as the observations indicated, instruments powerful enough could see it already. With passing time, the light would become brighter; after a while, visible to the naked eye; later, inescapable. And behind it were likely to come other phenomena more dangerous: a hail of high-energy particles and electromagnetic radiation whose effect on our planet would be incalculable. That, indeed, was the problem. The effects literally could not be calculated. There were no precedents, and too many unknowns. At one extreme, some theorists expected our atmosphere to be torn away, and all life to be extinguished. At the other, some claimed that interstellar gas along the path of the advancing wave would act as a shield, and the effects of the radiation particles be minimal. Needless to say, there were various positions in between.

There remained the matter of breaking this news to the world. When? A point would come, if the astronomers' predictions were correct, when the world could hardly, on its own account, fail to notice. Charlie's first calculations, made in his room at Siding Spring, had led him to expect no more than a few days. Consultation with colleagues more up-to-date in certain fields than he, had led to a revision of these figures. On the best evidence now available, it looked as though, for about one hundred days, there would be no way for the world – other than the world of major telescopes – to know what threatened it. Then – about mid-February – the light would brighten. It would begin to look like a planet. By late February it would look like Mars – Mars in the wrong segment of sky. Every amateur with a passing interest would see it, and ask questions. By mid-March, it would begin to illuminate the night sky: a pin point of light (technically) but as bright as the moon. Then, within two or three days, the particles would come.

So – what was to be done? There were, as the Chair pointed out, no precedents. No, thought Charlie. At least, not in the records of the United Nations. Ragnarök, perhaps? Or the Book of Revelation? Maybe it was time the diplomats turned to the seers. Or the prophets.

Various delegates went to the rostrum. There were questions. Reactions. Suggestions. Most of the presentations were low in key. They represented various conflicting interests and ideologies – Communist and Capitalist, developed and under-developed, Eastern bloc and Western, Islamic and Third World. The rhetoric varied. But it seemed to Charlie, as he listened, that the burden was constant. Every speaker was invested in the same thing. Panic must be avoided. It was too soon to terrify the world. If the interstellar gas theory were correct, very little would happen anyway. It would be best, for the moment, to do nothing. Just a few speakers broke the prevailing mood of calm. These expressed anger, attacking the credentials and integrity of the astronomers themselves. Two (from the Eastern bloc) claimed that the capitalist governments had distorted the evidence. Another (from the West) seemed to think that the report was a communist plot, designed to disrupt the free world's economy. Yet even the message of these came in the end, so far as Charlie could see, to the same thing. Nothing should be done. The scientists' predictions and fears should be noted but, beyond that, no action should be taken. And, most certainly, the world should not be informed.

But later? If the environment began really to disintegrate? If a moment came when the world began to see for itself? The question was raised once, only to be dismissed. This was a problem that the delegates were clearly not ready to examine. Perhaps that was why they were calm, or else dissipated emotion in irrelevant politics. What they chose to contemplate was relatively trivial. What was not trivial, they did not choose to contemplate.

Charlie was depressed. In his view, the interstellar gas theory was a thing of straw, clutched at because it was needed. *Humankind cannot bear very much reality*, he quoted gloomily to himself, and sat back in his place. Another delegate was making his way to the rostrum. Charlie's eye strayed once more to Jacqueline Austin. She scribbled a note, turned (so that, almost, he could see her profile), and passed the paper to a colleague who glanced at it, and shook his head. Charlie had the impression that she was frowning, though he could not see her face. What he could see was her mop of honey-blonde hair. That, and her shoulder. She was wearing blue.

Movement. A rustle of papers. Restrained conversation. The session had ended. Charlie hastily pretended to gather papers of his own, reflecting as he did so that having been sent here by Her Majesty to plan the end of the world, he had actually spent the last five minutes contemplating Jacqueline Austin. And her not even a British subject! Well, so be it. She did have beautiful hair, and that was a fact. Not even the threat of Final Judgement could change it. Nor, so far as he could see, would Final Judgement want to.

After the session, inevitably, there was another meeting of the British delegation, at which they all solemnly agreed that there was no more information to be shared, and nothing, for the moment, to be done. Charlie found his frustration mounting. He could not, honestly, see what he contributed by being there. And God alone knew what it had cost to bring him. Was this how *all* governments spent their money? But he was chiefly aware of increasing discomfort at the easy assumption that secrecy must be maintained – and tried to say so. Certainly, he could see the folly of dropping this news like a bombshell on an unprepared world. Yet the diplomats seemed still to be treating it as all part of the international game. For himself, he had always been clear that if a doctor knew he was going to die, he expected to be told. There were things he would like to do. Reconciliations he would like to make. Only thus could death be a human act. What then if the race were likely to die? Was no one going to consider giving it a chance to prepare? To think? To repent? Apparently not. It didn't accord with protocol. Or something. And in any case, it was a political decision, not scientific. He should leave the matter to experts, who would consult him when they needed. The matter was not put so bluntly. Indeed, everyone was quite insufferably polite. But the message was clear. His point was not taken, and the moment passed.

Eventually, they emerged. The first person he saw (perhaps because he was looking for her) was Jacqueline Austin with the other Americans. They seemed, like his own group, just to have finished. And now, come what may, he was going to talk to her. Excusing himself briefly to his companions, he crossed the hall.

She was by the coffee machine.

'Hello,' he said.

She looked up, surprised – then smiled. 'Well, hi! So you're a mysterious British diplomat as well as a great astronomer!'

To his embarrassment, he found himself blushing.

'Not much of either, I'm afraid,' he said. ('What a stupid remark!' he thought to himself. 'She'll think I'm a complete idiot.')

'Well anyway – welcome to Doomwatch. Hey guys, this is Charlie. He's a friend.'

Chapter Four

Back to Normal

Charlie Brown had been working with the team at Siding Spring as part of a leave of absence granted him by the University of London, where he was a senior professor. That leave ended in mid-November. The Foreign Office saw no reason why he should not return to his usual pursuits on schedule. Indeed, they encouraged it. So, he did; and after about ten days, began to feel that perhaps he had been rather hard on the diplomats.

The fact was, he didn't really believe it himself.

He remembered an older friend of his who had been in naval landings under fire during the second world war. Mates dropping all round you, he'd said: but somehow it wasn't as frightening as you'd expect *because it was always someone else who bought it, never you*. 'A thousand shall fall beside thee, and ten thousand at thy right hand, but it shall not come nigh thee.' The ancient fragment of messianic promise flowed into Charlie's head and out again. Well, it was like that now. Cosmic explosions. Suns and systems wiped out. That happened to other planets. One observed it all the time. But not to this one. Not really.

The data remained, understood by him better than most. But then, so did the determined normality of everything round him. He was teaching his usual classes. He was attending (as usual) too many committees in the Senate House. He was taking the tube every evening to Edgware Road Underground Station, buying a paper, and walking from there to Park West Mansions where he shared an apartment with his mother. How could such robust earth be about to melt?

Yes. Perhaps he had been rather hard on the diplomats.

Once or twice, the thing did come home to him. One Saturday morning in the park a child ran up to him, mistaking him for her father. She was a pretty child, and suddenly he realized that, if his calculations were right, she would never become a woman. There was a moment at the shopping centre, where he had gone to look for Christmas presents. He became aware of the hurrying hundreds. The ghastly shopping centre music (Christmas carols, Tijuana style) bore in upon him –

Hark (boom) *the herald* (boom) *angels sing* (boom) *Glory* –

and in an instant he felt his throat tightening, tears welling in his eyes. Glory? What glory? Look at us!

But most of the time, he didn't feel like that. Most of the time, the threat they had seen at Siding Spring and discussed in New York simply did not seem real.

There was, to be sure, another factor, complicating his responses.

He was in love. And such is the absurd nature of human chemistry that everything else, including the imminent destruction of himself and the world, faded into insignificance before it.

Charlie's upbringing, although not unhappy, had certainly been somewhat isolated, at least from the opposite sex. His father had read modern languages at Cambridge, married on graduation, and then been conscripted for National Service. On Saint George's Day 1951, whilst serving with the first battalion of the Gloucestershire Regiment, he had been killed on a hillside in Korea, so contributing to the long tale of that regiment's glory, and leaving Charlie's mother a widow at twenty-four. He never saw his son. They had few relatives and she, no doubt understandably, inclined to overprotect her only child.

Society colluded, at least so far as exposure to the opposite sex was concerned. From the age of ten, when Charlie went to the local boys' grammar school, the setting of his education was celibate. His teachers, rightly perceiving his above average intelligence, encouraged him strongly to spend his evenings in study rather than more sociable pursuits. His diligence, and theirs, was rewarded in time by an open scholarship to Keble College, Oxford – at that time, a male preserve. In his middle year as an undergraduate, he became a Christian; but his conversion centred on Pusey House which was then, like his school and his college, an institution only for men.

It was not that he was unattracted by the opposite sex. It was simply that when he graduated at the age of twenty-two life had scarcely given him opportunity for the kind of experience and encounter that most people have by fifteen. The problem was compounded by a shyness that made it hard for him to impose himself where he was unsure of welcome, and a fastidious pride that made him reluctant to make a fool of himself. So, though once or twice he was sufficiently attracted by an undergraduate of one of the women's colieges (at that time a tiny minority) to make some approach, he was generally too shy to be effective, and his pride too great to allow him to persist through real or imagined rebuff. So he had proceeded through life into his early thirties, over-intelligent and emotionally immature, a brilliant academic success and a disaster (he reckoned) at everything else.

But now, for the last forty-eight hours of his stay in New York, he had spent every possible moment with Jacqueline Austin. They had talked. Indeed, Charlie Brown being Charlie Brown, they had done little else. ('*Not* a fast worker!' she had chortled to herself as he went to get her another cup of Sanka.) For once, it did not matter. As it happened, Jacqueline Austin had been hurt rather badly by lovers whose ardour, it seemed, blazed with bright self-confidence until she returned it, and who then withdrew. From her own pain she was perhaps able the more easily to perceive Charlie's genuinely affectionate nature; and her experiences of those others so much more efficient than he in the art of courtship inclined her to be patient, and even to take a degree of pleasure, in his somewhat Victorian advances.

So, they talked. But they talked well. About Siding Star and its effects, naturally. Both being bound by their governments to absolute secrecy, it was good for each of them to have someone sympathetic in whom to confide, without betraying confidences.

As they sat together in a quiet corner of the coffee lounge, away from the other delegates, he told her of his fears.

'You don't think much of the "interstellar gas" theory, then?' she asked.

'No,' he replied. 'I don't. I wish I did. I hope it's right. But I very much doubt it.'

'What do you think will happen?'

Desire to prevaricate strove with training, and training won. 'I suppose I don't think there's a lot of hope. For survival, I mean. There might just be a chance in Northern Scotland. Or Canada.'

'Why? What's special about them?'

'The southern hemisphere is facing the explosion, more or less. It'll get the full impact. The northern part of the northern hemisphere's comparatively shielded. Think of throwing a bucket of water at a tennis ball. The side of the ball opposite from where you threw just might stay dry.'

'Will you go up there?'

'No, I don't think so.'

'Why not?'

'Well, for one thing, I don't think it's worth it. For another, I'm not sure I want to survive the rest of the human race.' (He almost added, 'Certainly not you,' but was not yet bold enough.)

'Yes,' she said. 'I think I see what you mean.'

He also told her of his frustration over the delegates' general failure, as it seemed to him, to face the thing at all.

She smiled. 'Well – sure – there was a lot of regressive behaviour around. That's what you were up against.'

'What do you mean?'

'Well – the fact is, you and your friends have faced us with annihilation. The basic, original, crown-it-all dread. And we handled it like we were programmed for a Melanie Klein textbook. Some of us went all paranoid-schizoid – which means, project your anxiety onto the nearest handy object (in this case, our favourite bunch of astronomers) and clobber it. Those were the guys who called you commies or capitalists or whatever they didn't happen to like.'

'And the rest?' he asked.

'The rest of us really refused to admit the danger exists at all. "A magic denial based on fantasy" – that's what it's called in the trade. And that's what you saw. It's sad if you're involved – as I am. Clinically, I guess it's interesting. Such a large group. So many cultures and so sophisticated.'

There was a pause.

'Mind – I guess you could say we've been showing the same symptoms in dealing with nuclear weapons for years . . .' She paused again, thoughtfully.

'Well, you enlighten me,' said Charlie, 'though you don't exactly cheer me up.'

She met his eye.

'Don't be too hard on us,' she said. 'Just imagine what it's like being in their shoes. That's why they need people like me. You really need a knight of faith to cope with all this – like in Kierkegaard – and I guess we just don't have too many of those.'

'Of course you're right,' he said. 'But it's depressing, all the same.'

She looked at him whimsically.

'Come,' she said at last, standing up. 'Let me show you something.'

He followed her curiously through the complex, and even so was taken aback by the place to which she brought him. A place of stillness. At the centre, an uncarved block, lit by a single beam of light. No other symbol. Yet the air was calm, and there was hope.

'You see?' she said softly. 'The Meditation Room. Dag Hammarskjöld designed it. He was a knight of faith. And he was part of all this. Don't forget it!'

Charlie was suitably chastened.

She smiled gently.

'He was also a scourge of psychologists,' she added. 'D'you know what he said about us?'

Charlie shook his head.

'He said we've made it too easy to dismiss the perplexing mystery with labels that put it in the category of mere aberration. So – if you catch me at it – tell me!'

It was Charlie's turn to smile.

'I don't think you do that too often,' he said.

But they had talked about other things than the United Nations and Siding Star. They talked about her mother and father and sister in Charleston, South Carolina. About his mother in London. About Oxford, where Jacquie, having graduated *summa cum laude* from Harvard, had spent a delightful first year of post-graduate study before returning to Harvard. About politics. Even about God. Amongst other eccentricities, Charlie had retained from student days his Christianity, somewhat to the scandal of several of his university colleagues. There had been, indeed, a famous coffee break at Imperial College, London about two years previously, when a group of them had publicly challenged him upon the subject. The ensuing debate, before an assembly of fascinated spectators, had lasted until lunchtime, at the end of which it was generally agreed, even by the indifferent, that whilst Christian orthodoxy might remain a minority taste, if you proposed to attack it in the presence of this particular professor, you had better get up early, and be sure you knew what you were about. Needless to say, for Charlie to discover that Jacqueline Austin was an Episcopalian, and even shared with him a delight in C. S. Lewis, merely added one more detail to her already sizeable catalogue of perfections.

After about twenty-four hours of this (between committees, with which they were both burdened) she took him to visit relatives (on her father's side) who lived near the Cathedral of St John the Divine. They were a delightful, chaotic family who took him to Evensong, gave him a tour of the Cathedral, introduced him to the Dean *and* a local Rabbi, and finally filled him with sandwiches, cake, and tea. ('All Englishmen drink tea,' they said – so of course he did.) Thus presented to a part of her family, even Charlie Brown was not so lacking in self-assurance as to avoid the conviction that she must at least like him. So, he was at last bold enough to hold her hand; then, when it was time for him to leave, he asked her to come with him to the airport and she agreed; finally, when he must say 'Goodbye' and enter the Departure Lounge, he totally exploded his own universe by putting his arms round her and kissing her – clumsily, to be sure, and almost losing his glasses in the process – but then, he was not very experienced.

'Why don't you come to Charleston for Christmas?' she said, still in his arms and making no attempt to move.

His face dropped.

'Oh Jacquie, I'd love to. But I must spend Christmas with Mum. I really must.'

'Okay,' she said. 'I guess it's a bit soon to ask your mum too. Well, why not come in the New Year?'

'Right!' he said. 'I will.'

He was passing through the gates, when she called his name. He looked back.

'Hey! Stay healthy!' she said.

He grinned. 'All right,' he replied. 'But I think I may need a psychologist.'

Which was, as we have said, one reason why the end of the world seemed quite a little thing.

Provided it didn't happen before the New Year.

If Charlie Brown was able so quickly to be distracted from the prospect of annihilation, what of the world's governments, of whose representatives he had earlier been so scornful? To do them justice, it would by no means be true to say that all of them did nothing. Individually, many acted with remarkable vigour, generally taking steps to preserve at least what they regarded as the brightest and best. Particularly was this true of nations whose territory stretched to the northerly part of the northern hemisphere, though it would be hard to say whether this was because they had access to areas thought to give the best chance of survival, or because of a tendency in those cultures not to give up without a fight.

At any rate, government offices and government servants found themselves called upon, without warning or explanation (or, at best, with flimsy excuses – 'for an exercise', 'in the event of hostilities') to produce contingency plans for the selection and movement of significant groups; for the swift creation of underground complexes – schools, hospitals, administration; for the commandeering of transport. From the *Politburo*, controlling agency of the Soviet Union, orders went out for the rapid extension of various northerly bases, and for the immediate transfer of vast supplies of food and technology. Military manoeuvres in and around the Kola Peninsular were announced on an unprecedented scale for February 'until further notice', and it was significant that the normally (and understandably) sensitive Finns for once made no protest. In another part of the hemisphere, the Canadians and the United States co-operated magnificently. The Canadians received resources and technology. The United States leased space. Discreetly, there was movement northwards. Underground complexes were constructed in Canada and Alaska – little different from their Soviet counterparts.

Exactly similar patterns might have been observed in some of the smaller countries – Britain and her Scandinavian neighbours, for example. In London, liaison between the Ministry of Defence and the Department for the Environment was remarkable. Sir Charles Dancy's minions presented their scenario, and at once, since it offered a ray of hope, the northerly part of the British islands was important. An operation was mounted – codenamed, in all documents, by the single word 'Deliverance'. Crack units – the SAS and the SBS, and the cream of the RAF – were moved to the far north. There was the usual excavation and construction, on a large scale. And budgets were suddenly unlimited.

Naturally, all this activity could not go unobserved, particularly in the democracies. Questions were asked. But the explanations were ready. New refineries. New bases. A new mine. Contingency against nuclear war. Only with time could it become apparent, to those with access to information and tools to analyze it, that the scale of the operations went beyond anything that the explanations explained. Only with time – and time was not on the side of the questioners.

Other governments, to be sure, did nothing. These resolutely fixed attention on their usual concerns, and so followed in both letter and spirit the recommendations of UNSELC. For them, essentially, business was as usual, and all else illusion.

Whether, in the last analysis, there was any real distinction to be drawn between those who pretended Siding Star was not there, and those who plunged into activity because of it, may be doubted. For the implications of the facts and figures which the scientists had provided were plain. Barring a miracle, the greater number of planet Earth's inhabitants were doomed. The real task, therefore, was to prepare humankind for death. For Charlie Brown's avoidance of the issue there was, as we have said, a reason, however absurd. He was in love. And perhaps, after all, this was not so absurd, since love is, just possibly, the one thing in life that is more important than death. But so far as could be seen, the governments of the world were not in love. Their problem was as Jacquie Austin described it. They contained but few who were knights of faith.

Chapter Five

The Flight

November passed into December. Everywhere, it was a hard winter. Conditions in areas above latitude 58° North were generally appalling, but the excavating and the building went on despite all obstacles – in Murmansk and Fort Wainwright, Scapa and Fort Simpson.

Charlie Brown in London continued along his usual paths (as advised by the Foreign Office), and continued in love. Aside from love, his biggest disturbance during these weeks was that, for an administrative reason which he could not fathom, the University of London decided to begin the Christmas vacation a week earlier than originally announced, so disrupting his and everyone else's timetable. He surmounted the disorder, using the unexpected free time to review a couple of books, and to proof an article dramatically entitled 'Assessing the Age of Large Magellanic Cloud Blue Globular Cluster NGC 2134' for *Publications of the Astronomical Society of the Pacific*. Later, he went carol singing with the church choir and attended midnight mass. A telephone call from Jodrell Bank, and a couple of summonses to conferences at the Department of the Environment reminded him that Siding Star was still there. At both these conferences, he met with representatives from the Ministry of Defence. His opinions and advice were sought, but he was told nothing. At one of them he also met Sir Charles Dancy, and rather liked him. From time to time he and Jacquie spoke to each other on the telephone, but they seldom mentioned the star. His mother thought it very adventurous, his having a girlfriend in New

York. (Privately, she couldn't see it working.)

Three times in six weeks, he dreamed the Dream.

New Year came. After a seven-hour flight from London, Gatwick, Charlie found himself on Concourse A at Atlanta Airport, waiting for Delta Flight 285 to Charleston. A three-hour stopover at Atlanta is perhaps not the most boring experience in the world, but must be near it. He had finished his book, and did not feel like reading it again just yet; so there was little to do save sprawl uncomfortably on a plastic seat, and endure the taped music. With the aid of daydreams about Jacquie, an abandoned copy of *USA Today*, and a magnificent 95-cent cone from 'The Ice Cream Shoppe', he survived, and at last they boarded the aircraft.

'What,' he wondered as the Boeing 727 banked and climbed, 'if the engines stopped?' They didn't. Instead, the pilot wished them a pleasant flight and the stewardess talked about safety equipment whilst nobody listened. Then the hostesses brought them soft drinks and nuts to sustain them through the fifty minute journey. 'You get better nuts on Belmont,' remarked the man on his left to no one in particular. 'Only trouble is,' he added, 'to get them you have to fly Belmont.'

As the drinks trolley wheeled past for the last time, Charlie noticed miniature bottles of spirits lining the centre. Presumably for the real he-men to drink. How, he wondered idly, did one say 'he-man' in inclusive language? (His department had recently circulated a memorandum on the subject.) 'He-person?' That was ridiculous. Unless, of course, you conceded that 'he' was no longer a masculine personal pronoun, but simply an adjective denoting aggressive characteristics and applicable to either sex. In which case it might be acceptable? Abruptly, he felt the thud of wheels hitting tarmac. They had landed.

As the aircraft taxied, Charlie panicked. He had flown several thousand miles for this: but what if they didn't still like each other? What if it was all a mistake? The seatbelt sign was off and the aircraft was still. Feeling slightly sick, he got to his feet.

Leaving the aircraft cheered him. It was pleasant to emerge onto a windy flight of steps where you could breathe real air, rather than (as at Atlanta) being passed along a giant plastic tube from one artificial atmosphere to another. The sun was shining and there was a hint of breeze as he walked towards the small brick terminal, entering it through a gate on the right.

Bustle. Cries of welcome. Swinging doors and moving figures. But there, at the still centre, she had seen him. Honey-gold mop and gentle smile; white jeans and a soft white shirt. He knew why he had come.

Chapter Six

The Idyll

Charlie put down *The Lord of the Rings* and looked at his watch.

Six-thirty a.m. He was suffering from jet lag. By the time they had reached the Austin's house last night it had already been towards midnight by his inner clock. Adrenalin and good manners had sustained him for a while – long enough to meet Jacquie's parents and her grandfather, and what appeared to be an unending succession of variously sized dogs and cats. (Jacquie also had a sister, but she, he gathered, was at a friend's house.) The family fed him and flattered him, and he enjoyed himself hugely. But gradually exhaustion overtook him and, laughing at his drooping eyes, they put him to bed at 8.35 p.m., Charleston time. So he awoke (naturally) at 4 a.m. (which, taking one thing with another, was rather better than he might have expected) and passed the rest of the night re-reading *The Lord of the Rings*, thoughtfully provided in a bedroom bookcase.

He had just decided that it was still too early to get up, when there was a tap at his door, and Jacquie's voice. 'Are you awake?'

'Yes!' he said.

She came in and shut the door. She was wearing a blue dressing-gown. He thought he had never seen anyone look so beautiful.

'Hey!' she said softly. 'How are you doing? Shall I pull your blinds?'

'Fine! Yes – thank you!' He grinned at her – delighted, but feeling slightly foolish.

She pulled the blinds. 'Welcome to Charleston! It's raining.'

She came and sat on his bed.

'Well,' she said, 'what do you want? Coffee? Orange juice? Or me?'

There was only one answer to that, and he gave it.

A minute's bliss was ended by a thud at the door.

'C'mon Jacquie! I know you're in there.'

'Oh dear,' she said. 'The joys of sisterhood. Go away!' she called out. 'You can see him later.'

There was a pause, then a banging of what sounded like pans, and an off-key voice singing –

'God save the gracious Queen,
Long live the noble – '

Jacquie leapt off the bed, shot across the room, and flung open the door – five-foot-four-inches of blonde fury.

'Susanna Austin,' she said, 'that is *pathetic*. What's more it's DAM' RUDE.'

There was silence, then an embarrassed muttering.

'Well, all right then,' said Jacquie, and came back, closing the door firmly behind her. She looked at him and laughed. 'I guess you'd better settle for coffee,' she said. 'We'll have no peace till she's met you. You've got to understand, an Englishman in this house is an event. She can't make up her mind whether you'll be wearing a red coat and carrying a musket, or being politely heroic like David Niven.'

'Oh,' said Charlie. 'I'm not sure I can live up to either.'

'Don't worry,' she said. 'Just talk in that gorgeous Limey accent, and she'll go weak at the knees. Like I do. Don't be long!' She kissed him lightly, evaded his grasp, and left.

About twenty minutes later, showered, shaved, and in his right mind, he emerged – to be at once addressed by a very pretty girl, aged about twelve, and obviously Jacquie's sister, who was hanging over the banisters.

'Hi!' she said. 'I'm Susie Austin. I've got to apologize because I was *extremely* rude.'

He grinned. 'Oh, that's all right,' he said. 'I hardly noticed.' Which, under the circumstances, was ridiculous: but well-meant, and so taken.

'Hey!' Her manner changed abruptly and she addressed him in a conspiratorial whisper.

'Yes?' he said, automatically adopting the same tone.

'My sister Jacquie must be crazy about you. She *never* gets mad.'

Thus informed, he went down to breakfast.

Jacquie and Charlie now spent what both confessed to be the two most delightful weeks of their lives, enchanted with each other and free, within the limits of the Austin's easy-going family routine, to enjoy their enchantment. Having talked once of Siding Star, early in his visit, they did not talk of it again. So, though the knowledge was there, lying between them and affording, had they considered it, an additional bond, they went some way with the front of their minds to forgetting it. No doubt they were assisted in this by good health, good food, and love.

The Austins lived in Water Street, in a beautiful but dilapidated old house that Mrs Austin had inherited, together with an ancient lineage and not much else. Mr Austin was a Yankee, with connections in New England. It soon became evident to Charlie that Jacquie was the strong one of the family. Her mother was in poor health, and her father appeared overworked and tired. Her younger sister, though sweet, was hardly of an age to bear any burdens. So, though Jacquie's work with the United Nations kept her based in New York, she came home at every opportunity.

On most days, Jacquie and Charlie went out, wandering hand in hand through elegant streets in the mild January sunshine, or going further afield in an ancient Buick that took them on one day to Beaufort, and on another to Savannah, Georgia – whence they returned, exhausted and happy, at two o'clock in the morning.

On the fifth day, it rained again, so at Jacquie's suggestion they explored the attic. It was fun to discover relics – battered footwear that he called 'gym shoes' and she called 'sneakers'; her old tennis racket ('I was hopeless,' she said); and a pile of her school textbooks. By these revelations, she made him party to her history, and he enjoyed that very much. Amongst the textbooks they found a battered copy of Merrill's *Catullus*, at which discovery they were able to confide to each other that they had both been filled with romantic yearnings when reading *Quaeris quot mihi basiationes* at school. It drew near to lunchtime. Pleading a need to 'write something', Charlie escaped to his room, smuggling the *Catullus* with him. There, in feverish haste, he made a free translation for her, thanking heaven for Merrill's notes, which sustained his rusting Latin.

You ask how many times you'd kiss, 'ere I
Of kissing, Lesbia, took my fill:
Number the sands of Libyssa that lie
Along Cyrene's fruitful hill,
Between the oracle of burning Jove
And ancient Battus' sacred tomb; or write
The stars that see the stolen loves
Of men amid the silence of the night –
When you so many times shall kiss
Then that will be enough and more of bliss
For Catullus, love's loon:
In kisses then so rich,
Enquiry could not reckon them at all,
Nor evil tongue bewitch.

Reading it to her over their sandwiches and coffee was perhaps the most 'romantic' thing he had ever done. 'It's not very good,' he said. ' "Fruitful" is a bit feeble.'

'I think it's beautiful,' she replied, and kissed him – adding, with a shade more candour than tact, 'Anyway, it's the thought that counts.'

In the afternoon it was still raining, so with a grubby score that they had also found in the attic, they sang through *Trial by Jury*, assisted by a young man from next door who was hoping to court Susie, and the Doyley Carte Opera Company on the stereo. When the young man left (Susie never did appear) they listened in more sober mood to Vaughan Williams' *Fantasia on a Theme by Thomas Tallis*, with Leonard Slatkin and the St Louis Symphony.

'That was glorious,' said Charlie when it had finished.

'Yes,' she said. 'And chosen specially for you! Do you know what Herbert Foss says about it?'

He shook his head.

She fumbled for the record notes and found the place, her golden mop catching the light as she did so.

' "These nineteen folio pages hold the faith of England," ' she read. ' "In its soil and in its tradition, firmly believed yet expressed in no articled details. There is quiet ecstasy, and then alongside it comes a kind of blind persistence, a faithful pilgrimage towards the unseen light." ' She looked up, the light again gleaming on her hair. 'How about that?'

There was a pause. He found it hard to speak.

'Would you – walk with me towards the unseen light?' he said at last.

She nodded, suddenly serious. 'Of course. Aren't I already?'

He held out his arms. He was no longer clumsy, but ardent and beautiful. And nothing would ever be the same again.

During the evening, she had an irritation in her eye, and was obliged to remove her contact lens.

'You know,' said Charlie, as she blinked at him myopically, 'if I'd been asked who'd be my perfect fantasy lady, she'd be a beautiful, short-sighted blonde.'

She laughed.

'I assure you I'm quite real,' she said gently. 'And like it or not, a near-sighted blonde is definitely what you've got.' She laughed again. 'One thing though, darling – don't go round my office telling them I'm "short-sighted", will you? *I* know what you mean – but over here it generally means "stupid" – and I'm actually trying to convince them I'm rather bright!'

It was his last evening.

As they walked to the East Battery, they saw a harassed woman struggling out of a pick-up with parcels and a child. Jacquie went and helped her. Then they walked on, and came in silence to their favourite spot, looking south-west to Forts Johnson and Sumter, with the grey bulk of the USS Yorktown on their left. They stood by the plate that commemorates Charleston's rôle in the Revolutionary and Civil Wars. (Earlier in his visit, she had showed him with amusement the part that reads:

First Victory over the British	1776
Captured by British	1780

'The second bit we don't usually talk about,' she had said, 'but as it's you I'll let you see.')

For the first time in their relationship, they found it hard to talk.

'I'll tell you what,' she said abruptly, 'I've had quite a few crushes in my time – but the guys always lost interest. And I've had a few guys keen on me – but then *I* wasn't interested. I even had one guy I was keen on and he wasn't, and then later after college he turned up and he was keen and *I* wasn't. Can you believe that?'

Charlie laughed.

'But you, Charlie Brown, are the first man in my life that I've been absolutely crazy about who seems crazy about me. It's nice.'

He kept his arm around her more tightly.

'Look, princess,' he said at last. 'Whatever happens, I want you to know that as far as I'm concerned – quite selfishly – life's been worth it – just to have known you. What I said about walking with you – I meant it. You don't have to answer now – but let me tell you – if we come out of this, I want you to marry me, if you'll have me.'

'Oh, that's all right,' she said. 'I'm sure I will!'

Next day, he flew back to England.

Before leaving, he invited her to come to London. They agreed on the first part of March. It was the earliest date that was possible for both of them, but it was not without some sense of defying fate that they chose it.

Going through the departure gate at the airport, he looked back.

Involuntarily, her eyes had filled with tears. She raised her right hand in a tiny, mournful wave. Perhaps she had a premonition. At any rate, that last sight of her he never forgot.

Chapter Seven

Aarons

January. February. Charlie Brown taught his classes. Jacquie Austin counselled and consulted. Governments pursued their plans. And Siding Star drew near.

At last, as the astronomers had predicted, it became visible. Visible to the amateur's telescope. Visible to the naked eye. The world noticed. And the world wanted to know what it was. Official explanations were bland and reassuring. An unusual galactic phenomenon. A striking view of a supernova. Purely local in its effects. Unfortunately, in the Northern hemisphere, visible only in the early hours of the morning. But worth getting up to see, if you had the energy.

MARCH THE FIRST.

Chief Inspector David Adam was on the telephone.

He had arrived at Salisbury Police Station that morning full of bright feelings over the promise of his and Elizabeth's child; he had been pleasantly flattered by the good natured chaffing of colleagues to whom, on his wife's instructions, he told the news. ('I *don't* wish to be a closely guarded secret,' she said, 'and neither does Sproglet. Actually, we're rather proud of ourselves!') Then, as so often happens, he had found himself gradually deflated by a series of frustrations and irritations, of which the subject of his present conversation represented the most depressing.

'Look, Joan – you know and I know the bloke's guilty. And you know and I know what'll happen if we try to make it stick. She'll go through hell and humiliation in court, and at the end of it there won't be enough evidence to convince a jury. What do you *expect* me to advise?'

The voice at the other end seemed to be objecting.

'Well, yes,' said David, 'it sickens me too. But look at it. She invited him in and offered him coffee. *I*'m perfectly sure she just thought she was being averagely pleasant to the chap who'd come to deal with the power fault. I could have done it myself. So could Elizabeth – or you. But it makes no difference – the defence'll call it provocation and tear her to shreds.'

A further objection from the other end. David's frustration now showed clearly in both voice and manner.

'Well, of course that's true. But it's inadmissable evidence and you know it. So what the hell use is it?'

After a few more minutes, David ended his conversation, and replaced the telephone with a vicious crack that was reckless of government property, though it expressed well his feelings.

He hated and despised the advice he had just given. If it had been Elizbeth who had been assaulted . . . but he dare not think of it. Yet granted the system under which the law must operate – the need for proof beyond any reasonable shadow of doubt – he honestly did not see what else he could have said. The fact was, he was beginning to feel more and more the confusion of his whole job. Today's episode was simply an additional straw. Ever since the affair of the Academy, he had felt this disturbance. Event after event had pressed in on him the question – am I in the right place? Can I and should I continue doing this for much longer? In February there had been a case in which he found himself protecting the property rights of a man who appeared to be without morals or justice; yet the law was clear, and in the man's favour. A few weeks later, there had been an industrial dispute at a local factory; and police officers had been used in a way that made him distinctly uneasy. Now there was this morning's case. Perhaps irrationally, it seemed as if the promise of new life somehow precipitated the whole thing. It was like the beginning of an answer to his unasked question. Unasked – because he was still not entirely sure what the question was. He had not even been able to discuss it very effectively with Elizabeth. But he was sure of two things. First, that there was a question. And secondly, that as soon as the chance came, he would talk about it with Michael Aarons – and in this, Elizabeth encouraged him.

He looked at his watch. It was time to go home. Savagely, he gathered his papers together, threw some unwanted forms into the wastepaper basket, and went to take his coat from its hanger. He would be glad to get out of the place, even if only for a few hours.

Michael Aarons hung up his coat, gathered several letters from the hall table, and climbed the stairs to his study. A fire had been lit against his return, and was burning cheerfully behind the handsome fireguard. There were vases of fresh daffodils. His books and papers were as he had left them. The two big leather armchairs looked comfortable and friendly. He went to the window and looked out at the church, reflecting with pleasure on his weekend in Exeter.

The time with his friend had fallen not at all below expectation. Conversation had been as enjoyable as he had hoped, covering everything from theology to food, from choral singing to county cricket. They had walked on the cliffs near Branscombe, and scrambled along the beach, admiring rocks, gulls, and the surge of ocean. They had strolled in more leisurely fashion by Exeter Canal and they had enjoyed pints of Bishop's Best and hot pasties in the excellent Double Locks pub.He had learned with horror of a threatened development that would swamp the peaceful place with a 'restaurant complex', and gladly signed a petition denouncing such barbarism.

So the time had passed, splendidly enough. And yet, rather to Aarons' surprise, the service on Sunday morning – the ostensible purpose of his visit – had in some ways been its high point. Aarons was not a great preacher, and he knew it, but this time he had preached above himself. No doubt (he dutifully noted) he had been lifted by the Spirit; but the Spirit's instrument (or so he felt) had on this occasion been a remarkable warmth and quality in the group that faced him.

There had been an anthem – the first line of Psalm 133. *Hine ma tov u-ma naim, shevet achim gam yachad.* 'Behold how good and joyful a thing it is, for brethren to dwell together in unity!' The choir had sung the Hebrew words to the traditional melody – for Aarons, though they could not have known it, among the most haunting of all melodies, bringing back many memories of his Jewish childhood: the smell of his mother's fresh baked *challot*; the warm carvings of the old synagogue in Vienna; the lined and stricken figures of the deathcamp. What was truly amazing was that the melody had been set to a four-part harmony by the Musical Director – and so set that the arrangement seemed to Aarons to bring out everything that the melody meant to him: so enriching what he would not, previously, have believed could be enriched. It was well that they sang after Communion, when Aarons' active role in the service was over. If they had sung before he was to preach, he was not sure he could have spoken. As it was, he was able to recover in the silence.

Afterwards, he had met them, and the memory still gave him pleasure. It was not often he found himself addressing a young man who had played rugby for England, yet betrayed in conversation both humour and spirituality – being of the latter apparently quite unaware. ('How Anglo-Saxon!' thought Aarons to himself. 'They are always embarrassed to be saints!') Then – Aarons found himself chuckling as he remembered – there were the two delightful choirgirls who had entertained him until he (and they) could laugh no more with accounts of their teaching practice, and a dog called Montmorency. (That they should be talking of teaching practice in a School of Education seemed reasonable enough, but how Montmorency got into the conversation he could not recall.) Then he had met two splendid ladies – both teachers in the University – who between them found the chaplain's keys, prayer book, and service sheet, at various moments when it seemed that all might be lost. Finally, there had been the organist – a young man whose heartfelt professions of incompetence before the service convinced Aarons that they would be fortunate to get through at all, and who then performed with near brilliance. Aarons chuckled again.

He glanced at his watch. Half past twelve. The journey from Paddington had taken longer than expected. He wondered, idly, where Jim was. Probably in the church. Then he heard the rattle of the front door, and walked back to the stairs.

Down in the hallway stood Jim, wiping his feet (it was drizzling outside). He hung an umbrella on the brass coat stand by the door, and placed a length of cable and an inspection lamp on the hall table.

'The heating went off in church,' he explained, noticing Aarons' curious expression. 'It's all right. We had to poke about under the boards. But I think we got it right. It's on again for now, anyhow.'

Aarons beamed. Ever practical Jim! Officially, Jim was Michael Aarons' secretary, and secretary to the St Andrew's Foundation, but in addition to performing these tasks, he also possessed many other skills which Aarons admired. Aarons himself would have had no more idea what to do when the heating went off than he would have had the ability to fly. It was good to be back. It had been good to be away, but it was good to be back. He descended the stairs, went to the vestry, and put on his cassock. It was nearly time for the midday Communion. Then he went into the church.

Sir Charles Dancy sighed. Well, they had prepared the blighter as well as they could. It wouldn't be their fault if he went and muffed it.

Question Time in the House of Commons is one of the more amusing aspects of British Parliamentary democracy, whereby the mighty – that is, Her Majesty's ministers – are put on the spot. The ceremony takes place on Mondays after lunch, and since there is always the chance that a mighty one will look foolish, the House is generally crowded. It is, of course, the task of the civil servants in the Minister's department to see that the Minister, being properly briefed, does *not* look foolish: so a failure in this respect reflects badly, not only on the government, but also on the civil service and the department concerned.

Today it was the turn of Sir Charles Dancy's Minister to be on First Order at Question Time. Ministers were generally (it seemed to Sir Charles) hard to brief, but this one semed harder than most. Still, the Minister's Private Secretary, the Assistant Private Secretary, and a host of lesser civil servants had spent hours during the last few days preparing answers not only to the tabled questions (that was the easy part) but also to every conceivable and inconceivable supplementary (that was the hard part, for it is in the untabled supplementary that the true art and cunning of the questioner lies – an art and cunning that need not be revealed until the moment itself). All this they had done, and they had sent their Daniel to the lions' den as well prepared as they could. It remained to be seen how he would perform.

But as Sir Charles went to lunch, he had other concerns

besides the performance of his Minister. Of the civil servants in his department, only he was in a position to see that no less than four of the tabled questions had to do with Siding Star. Would the Minister explain why heavy building development was taking place at (here followed a list of sites) on areas specifically designated by the Minister himself (here followed a reference to Hansard) as areas set aside for conservation? And so on. The questioners themselves appeared not to have realized the connection of their questions with each other, or with Siding Star. Nor, Sir Charles devoutly hoped, would they. Once they did, there would be trouble.

Charlie Brown heard the church bell as he left Gamages store in Holborn, where he had been on a lunchtime errand. He looked up at St Andrew's clock, then at the church itself. He had passed it a thousand times, noting it as one of many fine churches in that part of London; but he had never been inside. Well, why not? Last night, for the second time in a week, he had dreamed the Dream. As usual, it had left him disturbed. Nor was this his only worry. During his last two or three conversations with Jacquie, she had sounded cool. He knew she had much to do, being hard-pressed both by her employers and her family. She was also trying to finish a piece of research. So the truth was probably that she was tired. All this he could well see. Unfortunately, in affairs of love, Charlie Brown was insecurity incarnate. With his intelligence he told himself that he could not expect even Jacquie to be meeting always his exact needs; but intelligence did not obliterate disappointment.

Yes. It would be good to spend a little time in quiet.

Tediously, he negotiated the Holborn Circus traffic, was sworn at by a motorcyclist, and found himself facing a handsome notice board. 'Holy Communion 1.10 p.m. Tuesdays and Thursdays.' Today was Tuesday. Very well.

He would attend.

He entered by the south entrance, looked around him in amazement, saw Michael Aarons in his black cassock, and fainted.

Chapter Eight

The First Conversation with the Archdeacon

Someone fetched Jim, and between them they easily enough had the young man propped up in a pew.

'Is he drunk?' said someone.

'Drugs?' said someone else.

Michael Aarons smelt his breath, then lifted an eyelid and looked at the pupil.

'Neither, I think. He's just fainted. Look, he's coming round.'

Charlie Brown blinked. Consciousness returned. He had been by the church door. Now he was seated. But how – ? He saw the face of the priest watching him. It was the face of the man in his dream. But now he dared look at it, and saw what he had not seen in the dream. It was a kindly face, not free of suffering, but with signs of wisdom and humour, too. Beyond it, others. And beyond them, the great hall – lofty pillars, cream and gold; magnificent black and white flooring, like a chessboard. St Andrew's, Holborn Circus.

'How do you feel? Are you all right?'

The priest was talking to him. Asking the questions anyone might ask. Slowly, it dawned on Charlie that he had fainted. He struggled upright, and the conventional reactions of one who hates to cause a fuss came instantly to him.

'I'm so sorry. I must just have blacked out. Stupid of me. Yes – thanks. I think I'm fine now. Maybe I could just sit here for a bit?'

'Of course you may. Unless you'd prefer somewhere

quieter. Would you like to go to the Vicarage? We're just going to have the service here.'

'Yes. Communion. Weren't you just going to have Communion? That's what I came for.'

Michael Aarons smiled.

'We were indeed going to have Communion. And if you're sure you are comfortable, we shall. Perhaps we can have a word afterwards?'

'Yes. Thank you. I'd like that.'

'Good. Jim – could you very kindly light the candles? We are a little late.'

Aarons went to the vestry. Charlie noticed that the cassocked figure walked quickly and lightly, like a younger man. Jim lit the candles. The small congregation went to their places – not without a covert glance at their new neighbour – and soon the service began.

As it proceeded, Charlie felt calm returning to him. There was something infinitely strengthening in the great words and the timeless actions. By the time of the consecration he felt recovered, and a few minutes later went up with the others to receive.

After the service he remained in his place, until the priest came back. He got to his feet, and held out his hand.

'Father – thank you for your kindness. My name is Charles Brown. I teach at the University.'

'And I am Michael Aarons.' Aarons gestured round the church. 'You can see what I do!'

'Yes,' Charlie replied. 'I think I need to talk to you. Do you have any time to spare?'

'Of course. Do you drink coffee? Have you eaten? Come to the Vicarage. Let's see what we can find.'

As Michael Aarons led the way through the church, Charlie realized that he was ravenously hungry. So he needed little persuading to the plate of sandwiches that was soon set on the table beside him in Aarons' study. The priest made up the fire, and having thus seen to their comfort, fetched his own sandwiches and coffee, and placed himself in the armchair opposite.

'Well, my friend. Here we are. What would you like to talk about?'

During the service, Charlie Brown had resolved to tell the priest about his dream. Yet now he came to it, the matter sounded preposterous, and he said so.

'Frankly, what I want to tell you sounds ridiculous. Sounds ridiculous to me, anyway.'

Michael Aarons grinned.

'In my trade, I'm fairly used to ridiculous stories. Try it. Why don't you tell me a bit about yourself first, though? Give your ridiculous story a background. If you like.'

Charlie liked. In fact, it made things a good deal easier. He was at least able to tell the priest enough about himself to suggest that he was not a half-wit. He told him something of his work, of his family, and even a little about Jacquie. Finally, he came to the Dream. Aarons bent forward, fingertips together, concentration complete. Charlie spoke of its recurrence in childhood, its declining frequency – and then its sudden recurrence of late. He described it.

'And the fact is,' he said, 'it's this church. And it's you. I've never been here in all my life before today. Yet there I was in Gamages, and the bell rang, and I walked across, and decided to come. And it's you. It really is you. In my dream, you are always telling me there's something I must do. That's the only difference. And in the dream it's frightening. Here, it isn't. But can you understand it? Or do you just think I'm balmy?'

Aarons questioned his visitor gently. About his childhood. About where he had lived. The possibility occurred to him that Charlie had been brought to the church as an infant, and carried some deep-down memory of it. Perhaps he had been frightened by a priest? But then, would that explain the young man's certainty that Michael Aarons himself was the priest of his dream? Another thought struck Aarons – the church itself had only been brought to its present beauty in the last decade. There was no way his visitor could have a *childhood* memory of the way it was *now*, save by prescience. Which brought them back to where they started. There was always, of course, the possibility that the young man was mad, or lying. The priest looked at him judiciously. On the whole, he did not think so. There remained, however, another factor, though touching upon it would be a matter of some delicacy.

'Powerful dreams,' said Aarons at last, 'whether they come from our own psyche or elsewhere, seem usually to be telling us about something that is important to us. Which means, if we are to understand them, that we must be prepared to face those things – all of them.' He paused, and looked sharply at his visitor. 'Come. Let us take each other seriously. May I risk something with you?'

'Of course,' said Charlie.

'Then I want to make a very impertinent suggestion. I want to suggest that a great disturbance has entered your life recently. I do not mean your love for your American friend. I mean something else. Something altogether less pleasant. A threat. A danger. Am I in any way correct?'

Charlie was shattered. Had he known Michael Aarons better, he would have been less surprised. As it was, he had skirted as well as he could round the affair of Siding Star – bearing in mind his pledge of secrecy – and was staggered to find himself so transparent to the priest.

'Well – yes – you're right. But I'm in a difficulty.'

Aarons waited.

'The fact is – I'm pledged. "Official Secrets Act." I've given my word. Signed a paper.'

Aarons nodded. 'That, clearly, is a very serious matter. Such a pledge is its own imperative. I certainly could not advise you to break it.' He hesitated. 'I refer, of course, to the *moral* aspect of it. Revealing the affair to me would also, presumably, involve you in a legal offence.'

Charlie, who had naturally taken some interest in the subject, assented. 'Yes,' he said. 'A misdemeanour under Section Two, I gather.'

'Exactly,' replied Aarons. He hesitated again. Then he said, 'Well, I only say this – there does seem to me to be a certain imperative about your dream also. And I have the feeling that your dream and your secret are linked. Only thus can I see why the dream should start to come again when the secret began to threaten you – which I take to be the case?'

Charlie Brown nodded.

'But you seem to think that your dream involves me. In which case, I think you may have to choose between what your pledge tells you to do, and what your dream tells you to do. I cannot tell you how to choose. But I think you may have to make such a choice. I'm sorry.'

There was silence.

'Look,' said Charlie Brown. 'I honestly don't know what to do. I must think about it. May I do that – and telephone you?'

'I think that is an excellent idea,' said Aarons.

The doorbell rang. 'There, I think, is someone I have promised to see.'

Charlie got to his feet.

'Now – are you quite sure you feel well enough to go out? You can certainly stay here longer if you need to.'

Charlie grinned. 'Oh I'm fine – really. I'm not usually a wilting violet. And I've got papers to mark, so I ought to be getting back.'

'If you feel sure,' said Aarons.

'I do. Really. And thank you – for everything. I'll think about this. And I'll telephone you.'

'Right,' said Aarons. 'I'll look forward to it. And in the mean time I'll pray for you.'

Chapter Nine

Aarons Reflects

Charlie went back to the University, and Michael Aarons went to his visitor – a young woman who had been commended to him by the Rector of St Dunstan's, Stepney. He spent an hour with her, then, after arranging to see her again in a week's time, took her to the front door and showed her out into the sharp, windy day. As often, he had found the time of counsel and prayer exhilarating rather than tiring. There was something about the sight of a troubled person struggling to be absolutely honest that never ceased to fill him with respect for the human spirit – even with awe. An old lawyer had once said to him, 'You know, Michael, you and I both have folks in trouble coming to see us. Often they've done wrong. Thing is – the ones who come to me generally want to know how they can get away with it. The ones who come to you want to know how they can be better people. It makes a difference!' Michael Aarons chuckled to himself. It certainly does, he thought.

Meanwhile, Aarons had problems of his own, to which, he decided, it was now high time he turn his attention. Seated at the desk in his study, he once more unlocked the drawer, and withdrew from it the manilla folder marked 'A.P.S.' He glanced through its contents, though they were well enough known to him. They were a record, so far as he had been able to make one, of the works and plans of the Academy for Philosophical Studies. By far the greater part was a long list of cases – suicides, breakdowns, and other ruined lives (none of them identified by name) – that had clear associations with the Academy. Aarons had gathered this list, not only from his own counselling experiences, but with the aid of colleagues who had also worked with the Academy's victims. It was a sad catalogue – and despite the efforts of Aarons and his friends during the previous All Hallows' Eve, it had continued to grow. There had been, indeed, an addition in the last week. The remaining contents of the folder consisted mostly of notes made in connection with the events of last October. There were also several newspaper cuttings, dated November first and second, referring to the fire at the Academy's premises; and there was a note of the Academy's removal to temporary premises in Hampstead, whilst the other premises were being rebuilt.

The priest frowned, then turned his attention to the cutting from Friday's *Times* that had most recently disturbed him. It had been on the 'educational' pages:

NEW COLLEGE IS CLAIMED AS MASSIVE BREAKTHROUGH

Minister of Technology has Words of Praise

Speaking at a dinner of representatives of the Managerial Institutes of Industry, the Rt Hon Robert Coleman, MP, Minister for Technology, referred in glowing terms to the massive breakthrough for Britain represented by developments such as the new Cranston College of Science in the heart of London's dockland. Here, he claimed, as a direct result of far-sighted government initiative, Britain had a chance as never before to take her place in benefiting from the advances of current technology. The new college was an outstanding example of co-operation between government, which had

> provided the basic resource, local authority, which had provided the site, and non-statutory bodies.
>
> The Minister referred in glowing terms to the contribution of the London-based Academy for Philosophical Studies, to whose credit must go the provision of considerable funding from voluntary sources. The new Institution would have a working association with the University of London. It was, said the Minister, in efforts like this, and not in the carping attempts of the opposition to make political capital . . .

And so it went on. Well, well, thought Aarons. Certainly all this would be as wonderful as the Minister said, if the leopard had changed its spots. That, however, was unlikely. And if not, then from the following October, an unspecified number of Britain's and the world's brightest young brains would each year be under the influence of an institution approved and supported by the same group that had tried to murder Elizabeth Adam, that was largely responsible for the catalogue of human disaster recorded in Aarons' file, and that had been willing to perpetrate the ceremony of the *Beriyt et-Mavet*: the Covenant with Death, that David Adam (and the wolf) had interrupted, barely in time, the previous Autumn. It was not a pretty thought.

As for Cranston College, Michael Aarons had heard rumours about it even before *The Times* drew his attention to its links with the Academy. There was, for example, the story he had heard a few weeks previously from a young priest in Limehouse. It concerned two young men – brothers, and parishioners – who had been working on the building site for the new college. Aarons sat back, and recalled the conversation.

'One evening over supper,' the priest said, 'they happened to tell their mother about part of the site being sealed off – no one allowed to go there because it was dangerous. An old tomb, or something like that, they thought – but the college authorities were very cagey. About a week later, the two boys were on their way out for a drink in the evening. "Don't you go getting into mischief," said their mother. "Stop fussing, mum," they said. "If you're not careful we'll go and start poking about that tomb." "Don't you go doing any such thing," she said, and off they went. Well – they went to the pub. That's clear. Several people talked to them. They had a couple of beers and then left at about nine. That's clear. And no one has seen them since.'

'What?'

'That's it. Vanished.'

'What about the police?'

'Notified, of course. And nothing. Nothing to suggest they went back to the College. But then – nothing to suggest anything. Complete mystery. But they had been talking about Cranston. What do you think?'

'Did the police check the site?'

'Oh yes, they went. Looked it over. But found nothing.'

'Hmm. The trouble is' – Aarons had been tired at the time, and perhaps that was why he spoke with uncharacteristic bitterness – 'as usual with these young people disappearing, there's nothing actually to go on. They may perfectly well just have decided to leave. For Glasgow. Or Timbuctoo. Thousands do.'

'I know,' said the young priest. 'The woman says she knows her boys. They wouldn't do a thing like that.'

'That's what they all say,' Aarons had responded tartly.

'I say it too,' said the priest, quietly.

Michael Aarons had felt himself properly rebuked. 'Thank you,' he said. 'Apart from anything else, I should not indulge in generalizations. I apologize.'

Aarons shook his head and sighed, recalling with embarrassment his insensitivity. Briefly, he prayed for the woman and her boys, and for the young priest. Then he returned to his file. The question was – when should he try to talk to David and Elizabeth Adam? In a few days, the college was to be opened officially. The first full intake of students was not planned until the Autumn, but staff would use the time until then for bringing the place to final readiness. In the mean while, fifty or so research and overseas students were being allowed preliminary use of some facilities. They were to be housed in one of the newly-completed residential blocks.

The opening itself promised to be a considerable occasion. There was to be a speech by the Minister of Education and another, in reply, by the Principal. There would be many distinguished guests, and amongst them, as a member of the local establishment, the Venerable Michael Aarons, Archdeacon of East London. The invitation stood, copper-plate engraving, gilt-edges and all, in the middle of his chimney-piece, causing him some amusement on account of its being addressed to 'Reverend and Mrs Aarons'. Should he wait to consult the Adams until after the opening? Until perhaps he had more to go on? Or should he do it now?

Suddenly it came to him. He would invite them to come to him as soon as possible for a weekend – which would be delightful anyway – and leave it to Providence when they could come. He looked at his watch. The chances were, they would both be out. But perhaps not. David being a police officer, and Elizabeth in Educational Welfare, neither of them worked hours that were completely regular. And he had a feeling that the sooner something was planned, the better.

He turned to the telephone, and dialled the Salisbury code.

Chapter Ten

The Telephone Call

The telephone rang.

'Blow!'

Elizabeth Adam stretched lazily across the sofa and picked up the receiver.

'Hello.'

'Is that you, Elizabeth?'

'Michael! How lovely! Hang on a minute!'

She put the telephone down, scrambled across to the television, and switched it off. As she did so, she noted that the bleak March day had turned to flurries of rain. Thank goodness she didn't have to go out. She went back to the telephone.

'How are you?'

'I'm well, thank you. How are you?'

'Oh, we're fine. David's out being the Great Detective, and I'm having an option day. We tried to telephone you last night. We've got news.'

'Oh, what is it?'

'Well – the fact is – you are talking to two people. Me, and Adam Junior, currently known as Sproglet. I am now Heavily Pregnant Liz.' (This was absolute nonsense, since there was, as yet, no sign of pregnancy in her appearance; but it was Elizabeth's instinct, on these occasions, to claim the most extreme before it happened.)

'Elizabeth, how marvellous!'

They spoke for several moments about her news, then –

'Well,' said Michael Aarons, 'I rang to give you an invitation. But perhaps you will be too heavily pregnant to accept it.'

'Good heavens, no!' said Elizabeth. 'We *love* invitations. Especially Sproglet. And now there are two of us, we outvote David. What is it?'

'I was wondering if you would all like to come and spend a weekend with me. Soon. I haven't seen you for ages – and, to be honest, I'd like to consult you about that Academy business again.'

'Yes, of course.' Suddenly, Elizabeth's voice was grave. The memory of the attempt on her life had continued to disturb her, and the news of the new life she now carried had seemed like a word of hope that might wash it away. It occurred to her that she had not thought of James Darrell once since she knew she was pregnant. Apparently, however, the past was not going to disappear so easily.

Michael Aarons heard the change in her voice, and wished he had not spoken.

'I'm sorry,' he said. 'That was stupid of me.'

'No,' she said, after only the briefest hesitation, 'it wasn't, Michael. Sproglet means hope. But hope doesn't mean pretending things didn't happen. It just changes them. What you said's okay. Hang on!'

She ran barefoot to the kitchen and found the big house-diary.

'Actually,' she said, picking up the kitchen extension, 'this coming weekend seems as good as any. You did say soon? After that, things seem a bit hairy for several weeks.'

'That would be splendid. Better than I dared hope. I'll just have to desert you for a couple of hours on Friday evening. Apart from that, we shall be fine.'

'Just to show you I *can* cope with mentioning the dreaded unmentionable – you wouldn't by any chance be going to the opening of Cranston College?' she asked.

Michael Aarons grimaced. 'How did you guess?'

'David read about the opening in the paper – and remembered our old friends at the Academy had some sort of an interest in the place. He saw it last year on a file, I think. Then you having said about the Academy made me think of it.'

'Elizabeth,' said Michael Aarons, 'you are remarkable. I should hate to try to deceive you.'

'Well, I suppose I do have a rather special interest. I'm not always quite so clever. By the way – does your invitation include Splodger? I think Pooh would rather stay with the neighbours; but Splodger hates to be left.'

'But of course!' said Michael Aarons. 'That is taken for granted. Her presence will be most important to us.'

'All right. I'll check with David as soon as he gets in,' she replied.

That evening, David Adam telephoned Michael Aarons, and confirmed their arrangement. As they talked, it occurred to Aarons that he might ask David if he had any thoughts about the two young men who had disappeared, or their possible connection with Cranston College.

David grunted. 'It doesn't sound hopeful,' he said. 'But I tell you what. I don't see why I shouldn't telephone the local police and ask how it's going. I dare say it's easier for me to do that than for you. And something may be coming up. You never know.'

'I'd appreciate that very much,' said Michael Aarons.

'By the way – there's something you could do for me,' said David.

'But of course,' responded Michael Aarons. 'What is it?'

'Well – when we're with you over this weekend, I'd like some time to talk with you quietly. It's something I'm trying to work out. And I'd like your help.'

'Then we must make sure that we have a time for that,' said Aarons. 'I look forward to it.'

By which request David Adam took a first step towards fulfilling his resolve to discuss his frustrations and his future with the priest.

Chapter Eleven

Charlie Brown Decides

Throughout most of the rest of the day, Charlie Brown wrestled with the question as to whether or not he should share the secret of Siding Star with Michael Aarons. He would have liked to telephone Jacquie and discuss the problem with her, but she was away on a conference, and could not be reached. The conference had been a last minute demand on her, and she had been obliged to call him from the airport to explain that she would not be able to keep their usual telephone date. She had sounded hurried – which she was. Charlie found himself wondering who else would be at the conference. The other members of the American delegation, whom he had met in New York? All of them seemed, in retrospect, to have been incredibly handsome, masculine, and above all, there. Abruptly, he told himself to shut up. She was, after all, coming seven thousand miles next Monday to see him. Deliberately, he returned his attention to his immediate problem.

Charlie Brown's word meant a lot to him. He was not of the stuff from which 'moles' and 'leaks' are easily made, and he struggled grimly. At 10.30 p.m. he went to bed, still undecided; and by 4.00 a.m. he was awake again, gazing sleeplessly at the ceiling. He looked at his watch, and a thought struck him. He got up, moving quietly so as not to disturb his mother whose room was across the hall, dressed quickly in a sweater and jeans, got his old Alvan Clarke six-inch refractor from the cupboard above his bed, and went up onto the roof. It was a fine night. And – yes. It had risen. A red star, barely above the horizon, but bright enough to be visible even through the London haze. He set up the telescope, adjusted the focus, and found himself seeing the star with an abrupt clarity that shocked him. Since last he watched it, it had grown, not merely in size, but in authority. It pulsed, slowly. He felt like Frodo in *The Lord of the Rings*, watching the Red Eye of Mordor. Siding Star. Death Star. Suddenly he could endure it no more. He told himself that haste was absurd, but dismantling the telescope he hastened none the less, and was relieved to return to the warm depths below.

He read until seven, then switched on the television. Breakfast news and chat was about all he could deal with. He fetched a glass of fruit juice and made himself a peanut butter sandwich. They talked to a beautiful actress who was opening in a new play. Then, as a fill-in before the main attraction (a newly-appointed minister), they produced an amateur astronomer who had 'views' about the supernova. Charlie leant forward, fascinated. Clearly, the man was something of a crank. More astrologer than scientist. He quoted the *Revelation of St John the Divine* (to the interviewer's evident amusement) and seemed to think that the new light in the sky was Lucifer come down to earth, having but a short time. He spoke of the nearness of the End; of a last chance for the nations to repent; and he had accurately observed that the new star was approaching from the centre of the galaxy.

The interviewer thanked him with polite tolerance, and passed on to the politician. Charlie switched off, and remained sitting in the armchair. He could hear his mother now, making tea in the kitchen. Yes – by twentieth-century standards, the man was a crank. Yet had he lived two hundred years earlier, he might have been called – and with justice – a seer. The fact was – leave aside the metaphysics – he had just about got it right. Charlie's own most sophisticated projection, based upon every resource of twentieth-century astronomy and mathematics, came to the same thing. The nations had a short time. What was more, crank or not, the man had correctly noted the key factor – the factor that had struck Charlie Brown from the first: *the thing was coming from the centre of the galaxy*. If he had noticed, how many others would? How many would have heard this morning's broadcast? And how long before others began to make similar predictions – more scientifically-based?

Suddenly, Charlie knew that his decision had been made. Almost, made for him. The governments of the world, who commanded him to secrecy, would soon have no secret to command. The veil was disintegrating as he watched. And that being so, he must surely follow, as Aarons put it, the imperative of his dream. Which meant – he must confide in Michael Aarons. The decision made, he felt better immediately. Certainly, it was a strange world he was entering. Yet it too was a world of facts. The experience of the Dream was a fact. Its coincidence with the coming of the Death Star was a fact. St Andrew's Church and Michael Aarons were facts. Lunacy or not – and had not that lunatic on television come closer to facing the truth than the delegates to the United Nations? – lunacy or not, he would confide in Michael Aarons. Somehow he did not feel that the gentle, somewhat pained wisdom of the priest would lead him far astray. He wished he could have shared his decision with Jacquie, but it was not possible. He must act alone. He was resolved.

He went to the telephone.

Chapter Twelve

Enquiries

Michael Aarons had jogged, showered, said morning prayer, and celebrated the seven-thirty Communion. He was glancing at *The Times* when the telephone rang.

'Hello. Yes. Good morning! Yes – of course. It's good to hear from you. No, not too early at all. Certainly you may. Just let me look. This afternoon? Two o'clock. Good. I look forward to seeing you. God bless you. Goodbye.'

Aarons scribbled a note, looked at his watch, and tutted. He was due this morning at the Board. He looked for a file he would need, and realized he had left it in the vestry. As he scampered past the kitchen, whence came sounds and smells of breakfast preparing, he paused and put his head round the door. 'Just going to fetch something from the vestry, Mrs Owens!' he said. 'I shall be straight back. Breakfast whenever you are ready, please!'

Sir Charles had cause for satisfaction. His Minister, taking one thing with another, had performed creditably. There had been a favourable reference in the nine o'clock news, and this morning's papers had also been polite. Unlike the Minister, who attributed the whole thing to his masterly handling of the House, it seemed to Sir Charles that they had got off lightly, Her Majesty's opposition being, for some reason or other, unusually docile. Still, Sir Charles was not going to complain about that. On the other hand, his feelings of satisfaction were by no means as unmixed as he would have liked. The fact that there had been those four questions on Siding Star remained. True, they had been answered (after a fashion) and nothing of significance had passed. But Sir Charles was beginning to wonder just how long the government's secrecy over the matter could be maintained. He too, by mere coincidence (for it was not his habit to watch television in the early morning) had seen the crank astronomer. He, like Charlie Brown, had felt the façade beginning to crumble.

Nor was he free from personal pressure. Though he did not place much personal credence in the theory that survival would be more possible in Scotland than in England, still, he would have liked, just in case, to move his niece and her husband and children – his only surviving relatives – up to the Highlands. Alas, it could not be. Sir Charles, though he would in no way have claimed to be a knight of faith, came of a school which, whatever its limitations, held to certain standards. Some things, such as using privileged information for personal or family advantage, were not done. And if a thing was not done, then Sir Charles did not do it. It was as simple as that. But it did not, at least in the short term, make his life any easier.

Later that morning, David Adam kept his promise and telephoned the Tower Hamlets police. His enquiries were not, it must be admitted, welcome. It was not just that the local force had, as ever, more than enough to do. The situation was worse than usual. The area had been inundated with a wave of crime, some petty, some serious. Muggings and street fights had become commonplace, and there were a couple of particularly unpleasant murders. As if to provide a backdrop of general disorder, tempers had been further frayed by a series of accidents and breakdowns. Four times in three weeks the electric power failed, once for several hours. A gas main leaked in Poplar High Street, and the area had to be evacuated for the day. Local telephones had become so unreliable, they were on the way to being a joke.

In this situation, it was perhaps not surprising that a rural colleague's enquiries about an obscure disappearance were not received with zeal. David persevered, and after a couple of calls, succeeded in speaking to one of the officers who had gone to the Cranston site. No, there was no more news. They were pursuing the usual enquiries. But there was nothing to go on, really. Cranston College? Yes, well, of course they'd had a look. No, there wasn't anything to see. Tomb? What tomb? Oh – the old site. Yes, well, they'd looked there too. One of the archaeologists had gone with them. Funny old chap. Said they mustn't talk in case they brought the roof down. They'd gone down some steps and found themselves in what seemed like a large hall. Very dank and dreary. Bits of stone lying about. And smelt rotten. Like fish gone bad. The old boy said afterwards it was something to do with the rocks. Nothing else there, really. And certainly no sign of any missing boys. All right? Not at all. Any time. Cheerio, then.

In the mean time, after reflecting on her conversation with Michael Aarons, Elizabeth embarked on a project of her own. She telephoned a friend on the staff of the *Salisbury Journal*, and got permission to call at their offices and read some files. She also postponed a couple of lunch-time engagements, and planned visits to the reference library instead.

Unaccountably shy about her researches, she did not mention them even to David. She did not, indeed, expect to learn anything of any great moment; but she thought she might learn things that would interest her, and even some that could be useful.

Chapter Thirteen

The Second Conversation with the Archdeacon

It was a fine day and Charlie, after an early lunch, was tempted to walk. On reflection, he realized that he didn't quite have time for that, and compromised by catching the tube as far as High Holborn. He then walked to Holborn Circus, enjoying the crowds and the delicate, chilly sunshine. As he reached St Andrew's, an enormous limousine, no doubt containing some civic dignitary, was just leaving through the green double gates that lead to the vicarage. Inside, Michael Aarons was standing in the midst of a group of several people by the south entrance to the church. For a moment, Charlie hesitated, but Aarons saw him, waved and smiled, and gestured towards the open front door of the vicarage. Inside, Jim was sorting letters on the hall table.

'Hello,' he said with a friendly smile. 'Father will be with you in a couple of minutes. He says would you mind waiting in his study? And would you like some coffee?'

'Thank you. I should like that very much,' said Charlie.

In the study, he found the fire burning brightly, and both armchairs occupied – one, by a magnificent persian cat who was asleep, the other by a bright-eyed tabby with a slightly frayed ear who looked at him curiously. Feeling he had no right to disturb either, he went and stood by the window.

He had arrived a few minutes early, and the hands of the church clock were pointing exactly to two when Michael Aarons arrived, still in his cassock, and carrying a tray with cups.

'Hello,' he said. 'It's good to see you again. But not standing! Albert! Marlene! What *is* going on? Do you occupy the best chairs – *illegally*! – whilst our guest stands? Shoo! Off!'

The persian jumped from the chair, oozing offended dignity, and stalked out of the room. The bright-eyed tabby sat up – and began to wash.

'*Albert*!' said Aarons meaningfully, and pointed to the floor. Albert, having shown his bravado to the world, took the point.

'I'm sorry,' said Aarons. 'I do hope you aren't allergic to cats.'

'Not in the least,' said Charlie, grinning. 'I like them.'

'Good,' said the priest. 'The fact is, I've a strict rule that they're *not* allowed on the armchairs. Needless to say, armchairs become the goal of all desire. Have some coffee. And if you're sure you're not allergic to cat hairs – have a comfortable chair. Good. Now. Let us talk. I gain the impression you have made a decision.'

'Yes, I have. I've thought about this as carefully as I can, and I think I must share my secret with you.'

Aarons nodded. 'Let me say then, for what it is worth, that I hear many secrets. Yours will go no further – at least, not without your permission.'

Charlie looked Aarons in the eye. 'I believe you,' he said, and began.

As clearly as he could, Charlie lay before the priest the story of the last few months – of the leave of absence that had been granted him by the University so that he might work with other British astronomers at the Siding Spring Observatory in New South Wales; of their concentration on a single segment of sky, and, through that, of their becoming aware, three months before the world could see it, of the phenomenon that was now attracting the world's attention. He told Aarons of the theory he had formed, and its subsequent support; and, finally, of his concern over international refusal to acknowledge the seriousness of the danger, or even to allow the world to know of it.

He spoke for nearly thirty minutes. His coffee grew lukewarm, untasted, and Aarons listened.

When he had finished, there were several minutes of silence.

'Do you believe all this?' said Charlie at last.

'Oh yes,' said Aarons promptly. 'I believe you. You are a person I should incline to trust anyway. But as it happens – I hope you will forgive me – I took the liberty this morning of asking a friend of mine in the University about you. I gather your description of yourself as 'teaching' erred only on the side of modesty. You are the Senior Professor in your department, and among the youngest ever to be appointed. In the field of galactic structure you are regarded as one of the top dozen people in the world. No, I do not think a person such as you would make this up. I believe you. And, of course, I had read for myself of the supernova, though I have not yet got round to getting up at four o'clock in the morning to see it. Look – your coffee is cold. Would you like some more?'

'Actually, I'd like a glass of water, if you don't mind,' said Charlie, for his long discourse had made him thirsty.

'That's easy,' said the priest, getting to his feet.

In a few minutes, Aarons was back from the kitchen with a glass of iced water.

'Of course,' he said, as he gave the glass to Charlie, 'I should be less than honest if I pretended that what you say is not personally threatening. Yet I do already know that neither I nor the world are immortal. I hope as a Christian I can deal with that. And maybe the end you think likely will be less unpleasant than the one we shall devise for ourselves, if we are left much longer.'

'There's something in that,' said Charlie.

'I think I understand your concern about when the world should be told – yet even there – well, all of us already know we are going to die and our time is short. The information is available.' He hesitated, then continued. 'But what does puzzle me is that if we are to take your dream seriously – and I feel we should – and if your dream is connected with Siding Star – and it does appear to be – then all this somehow links to me, and there is something that you must do. But how does it link to me? And what is it that you must do?'

'Frankly,' said Charlie, 'I haven't the remotest idea.'

Silence.

Michael Aarons sat gazing into space, turning over the story in his mind. It was surely as he had said. If they were right to take the young man's dream seriously, and if they were right to connect it with the threatened danger, there had to be a connection with Aarons himself. Something that concerned him? All right. Go from there. What was concerning Aarons at present? The Academy for Philosophical Studies? Certainly. Cranston College? Yes. Yet that seemed to involve a danger for the *future* of the world. How could it be linked with this threat of universal destruction *now*? The two contradicted each other. Was he aware of anything else that the Academy was up to? Those lists of personal disasters? Grim. But did they link with this? They seemed generally to be a result of the way the Academy functioned, rather than themselves a part of any plan or direction. The fact was, since the affair of the *Beriyt et-Mavet* on All Saints' Eve, he could think of nothing involving the Academy . . . Then, it came to him.

'When did you say this star was first seen?'

'November the first last. It appeared between 1.20 a.m. and 12.20 p.m.'

'Ah – wait a minute. Is that Australian time?'

'No,' said the astronomer. 'We don't work by local time.

It's too confusing. We work by Universal Time – UT. For all intents and purposes it's the same as Greenwich Mean Time.'

'So,' said Aarons, 'you are saying that it appeared at some time during the morning of November the first by the clocks here in England – by British time?'

'Yes,' said Charlie. 'You could say that. Why?'

The morning of November the first.

The morning of All Saints' Day.

The morning after David Adams had stopped the Ceremony of the *Beriyt et-Mavet* – the 'Covenant With Death'.

So perhaps there *was* a connection.

He looked at Charlie.

'I think I see it. But the boot is now on the other foot. It is I who have a pledge to secrecy. Over a very grave matter.'

He paused. Charlie watched him.

'Two friends of mine were involved with me on the night of October the thirty-first in an affair which might be linked to yours. I do not pretend to know how. I have only the coincidence of dates to go on; but it is a coincidence I can hardly overlook. My friends are due to come here on Friday evening.' Michael Aarons paused once more, then he continued. 'I propose this – I telephone them, explain that a very serious situation has arisen, and ask if they will be willing to share our secret with a fourth person – you. At the same time, I must ask if you are willing to share your secret with them. I give you my assurance they are a couple on whose loyalty and discretion I would stake my life. If you agree, and they agree, we must meet here on Friday evening for a council. If there is something to be done – and your dream suggests there is, then we are most likely to find it by pooling our knowledge. The first question is – will you agree to this?'

Charlie nodded.

'I agree,' he said.

Aarons looked at him again.

'To be exact,' he said, 'according to your dream, we have to find something that *you* must do.'

'Yes,' said Charlie. 'That's right.'

He paused. 'I've a late seminar on Fridays. But I think I can be here by nine.'

Chapter Fourteen

Disaster

Charlie walked slowly back to the underground station. Although he was sure that he had made the right decision – indeed, the only possible decision – he still found the prospect of Friday evening very threatening. The proposed meeting lay like a dragon guarding the gates of paradise – paradise being Monday morning, when Jacquie was to arrive on the overnight flight from New York. He realized that he was staring blankly at the man in the ticket office.

'Sorry,' he said. 'Single to Edgware Road, please.'

When he got back to the apartment, his mother was out. The telephone was ringing. It was Jacquie, rather earlier than they had planned.

She sounded harassed.

'Charlie,' she said, 'I'm sorry. I just can't make it. Not this time. My mother's illness has flared up again, and I *can't* just leave my pa to cope. I'll have to go there for my vacation. I'll just have to.'

That threatening light in the sky meant nothing. Charlie's universe had already collapsed. All his fears came screaming to the surface, and he felt physically sick. He scarcely heard himself saying, with a coolness he did not feel, 'Never mind, princess. If you can't make it, you can't.'

They chatted a little more, then said goodbye.

Charlie Brown now passed the worst night of his life.

The terrors of the Dream seemed to him child's play compared to the agonized frustration of his longing for Jacqueline Austin. At 3.00 a.m. he found himself weeping.

By 6.00 a.m. he had worked himself up to a resolution. It felt like being run over by a truck, but he had made it. The resolution was this – he had no right to be a burden on her. She had given him the most beautiful experience of his life. If she was growing tired of him (and God knew, why shouldn't she? – he could hardly count as much of a catch!) then she should be released from any sense of obligation and released handsomely. That much he owed her. What was more – if Aarons was right – if there was something he had to do about the Star, well, it might be anything. Perhaps for the moment he was not himself free to be involved in commitments. Not until this other thing was out of the way.

In such a mood, he telephoned her at her office next day in New York.

'Look,' he said, 'I want you to know you owe me nothing. If you're beginning to find this whole thing a bit much, that's okay. God knows, there's nothing especially marvellous about Charlie Brown to occupy the rest of your life. You've just got to say so, if that's what you want.'

There was silence from the other end of the line.

'Well, what do you want?' he said.

'What I want most in the world is just to be with you,' she said at last. 'That's what I want.'

He heard the words, but another concern had occurred to him.

'There's something else,' he said. 'Something's come up here in London. To do with Siding Star. Something I have to do. Until it's out of the way, maybe it would be better for us not to consider ourselves committed. Not for the moment.'

He went on to say at some length how important she was to him, and bade her goodbye.

'Goodbye,' she said.

'I'll phone you soon,' he said.

'Yes,' she said. 'All right.' She sounded puzzled.

The following extracts are from a document sent anonymously, twelve weeks after the events here recorded, to the editor of *The Observer* newspaper in London. Another copy was simultaneously received by a prominent London MP. The document is a photocopy on four sheets, from which the heading to the first and the end of the last have been removed. The subject matter does, however, have its own heading: 'House of Commons Select Committee on Domestic Affairs: Scottish Developments', and a reference number: MB 1286 5937 ME. In what follows, the head of Defence Secretariat II appears to be advising the Minister of Defence on how to reply to the Committee's questions regarding various developments in the area of Scapa Flow. The memorandum continues:

'We have discussed the nature and form of our reply with the defence commitments staff, DS6, and with ES5 of the Department of the Environment. On the basis of these conversations, our advice is that it would not at present be in the national interest to provide the Committee with a note giving full reasons for and details of the developments in question. First, in view of the Committee's terms of reference, such a note would have to be unclassified; but the details it contained would necessarily draw on Tactical Instructions 306, 307, and 308 which are, as you are aware, classified. In addition, full details would provide more information than Ministers are yet able to reveal about the scope and purpose of operation "Deliverance", this limitation on information having been also agreed with the United States' Government and the European Council of Ministers . . .' The memorandum goes on to list certain Commonwealth countries with whom special arrangements seem to have been made, including Australia, Canada, and New Zealand. It concludes, 'I therefore recommend that we should avoid all difficulties that will arise from a detailed reply to the Domestic Affairs Committee by providing it with a more general account.'

It was always open to the government to challenge the authenticity of this document, since neither the newspaper nor the MP could provide an original. On the other hand, the Select Committee's questions, and the Minister of Defence's replies to them, are a matter of public record.

Chapter Fifteen

Cranston College

The Adams arrived at St Andrew's on Friday amid a flurry of dog baskets and suitcases. Splodger rushed off at once with impertinence born of long familiarity to see if there was anything worth eating in the cats' bowls. The cats, to their credit, treated this disgraceful behaviour with dignified tolerance.

Michael Aarons was already dressed in his best clericals. His guests were properly impressed. Supper, explained the priest, was laid out for them in the dining-room. Everything, he trusted, was also prepared in their room. He expected to be back by half past eight. And there was time for an early glass of something before he went, if they wished. They did. David and Michael Aarons had sherry. Elizabeth looked ruefully at the decanter, and had orange juice. 'It's Sproglet,' she explained. 'Terribly puritanical about alcohol, you know. Won't touch it!'

In the study, whilst Michael Aarons was filling glasses, Elizabeth read the invitation. She grinned wickedly.

'There's a spare seat here,' she said pointedly.

'What did you say?'

'A spare seat. It says Reverend and Mrs Aarons.'

'Why? – Do you want to come?' asked Aarons.

'Of course I do. I'm madly curious. And think how much use I'll be as an extra pair of eyes. Spotting evil works. I expect I'll be much better at spotting evil than you, anyway.'

'Well . . .'

'You wouldn't mind being deserted for a bit, would you,

darling? An adventure for heavily-pregnant Liz.'

'I don't mind,' said David. 'It might be a good idea. An extra pair of eyes. I don't envy you those speeches, though.'

'There you are. Chief Inspector Adam says it's a good idea. How about that?'

'Well – I – er – I should be honoured. Why not?'

'Super. I'll change then. I don't suppose I'll go down too well in jeans. Can you give me fifteen minutes?'

'Easily. We don't have to be there until six. These things never start on time anyway.'

Elizabeth was half-way to the door, when conscience assailed her.

'I say, Michael, you're sure you don't mind? I mean – you weren't planning to go and be serious with Bishops, or something?'

'No, I did not intend to be serious with Bishops!' Aarons chuckled. 'You come!'

It was certainly a considerable occasion. A derelict site adjoining the College had been taken over for parking, and so great was the number of guests, it was twenty minutes before they were finally guided to a place by brusque, uniformed attendants. Five minutes' walk then brought them to the new building, where they had to wait again as a file of well-dressed worthies was slowly admitted. They passed through the 'reception area' (which seemed to substitute for the Porters' Lodge of older institutions) and so into an enormous, well-lit hall. The pause as they stood on the college steps had given them an opportunity to form impressions. The building was strikingly, even aggressively, contemporary. Passing through the transparent doors was like entering an air terminal. Money had been spent lavishly on the décor, creating an atmosphere of thick carpets, concealed lighting, indoor plants and ornamental running water. It was spacious, the temperature was even and, considering the crowds passing through it, the building was remarkably quiet. But somehow Elizabeth, at least, did not feel comfortable.

The assembly hall was arranged as one would expect for such an occasion – a platform and seats for distinguished visitors, microphones for distinguished speakers, and, facing them, several hundred seats arranged in rows for the less distinguished, amongst whom were Michael Aarons and Elizabeth. The fifty or so overseas and research students were already seated at the front. Other seats were filling rapidly. Michael Aarons and Elizabeth found places. A few minutes later, the assembly rose to its feet as the Principal entered with his guests – the Minister of Education, the Lord Mayor of London, Mayors of the East London boroughs, and a number of others whom Aarons did not recognize.

The first part of the proceedings – the official opening – was entirely formal. Proper things were said. Proper ceremonies were performed. Proper people were thanked. The Minister of Education said nothing in particular for about ten minutes. And the thing was done. Then came the Principal's speech. He was a heavily-built, slightly bulbous man in his fifties. He advanced upon the microphone as one who is aware of occasion, adjusted his papers, cleared his throat, gazed down upon the assembly, and began.

'Minister, My Lord Mayor, . . .' Aarons caught Elizabeth's eye, and winked.

The Principal spoke for nearly thirty minutes. His delivery was monotonous, and Elizabeth found herself drifting into reverie, centred upon the enormous indoor plant that stood in front of her. Why on earth could she not grow plants like that? She loved house plants. All her friends had them. She read books about them. Gave them plant food. Talked to them. Played music. Sang to them. And always the same result. Pathetic. Oh well. Some people could do it, and some couldn't. She obviously couldn't. Whoever grew that thing obviously could. It was gigantic. It was magnificent. It was . . . With disgust, she realized it was plastic. She glanced around her. Politely attentive faces. Glassy eyes thinking distant thoughts. Michael's face a mask.

The Principal appeared to be reaching his conclusion. He was speaking with fervour and perhaps just a shade louder than the circumstances demanded. She pulled herself together. This really was not good enough. She had practically made Michael bring her. The least she could do was pay attention. Now – what was he talking about?

'At this time, as never before,' declared the Principal, 'it is imperative that we be faithful to those principles which Life itself has placed so firmly in the grasp of our generation, for in them lies the key to Progress. First, as the Minister has so inspiringly reminded us . . .'

Was it really possible that this rather boring man, uttering platitudes and polite flattery, was the centre of a terrible plot? That his College was involved in a dark design? Or had her enthusiastic researches the previous week been part of a complete absurdity? She pursed her lips and frowned. That, after all, was what they were trying to find out. Hello – what was that? A ladybird was scuttling along the floor. How on earth had it got in here? The insect stopped; then turned irrationally. It was perilously near to a softly-tapping foot in the next row. Turn back, you stupid thing! Oh, no – it was actually going towards the danger! Ah – at the last minute it had spread its wings and shot away. Now where was it? On the wall to her left? Or was that a mark? She peered, trying to see if the mark would move. It didn't. Maybe the thing had got trapped in the air conditioning? Oh, no. Here it was again. What a stupid creature! A sudden burst of applause and a general relaxation of posture recalled her abruptly. He'd finished. And she'd hardly heard a word. The Principal sat down, mopped his brow and poured himself a glass of water. The applause continued as he drank it. Several of the audience rose to their feet.

'What did you think of that?' asked Aarons as they moved slowly out.

A momentary temptation to prevaricate was resisted.

'Michael,' she said, 'I'm ashamed. After all the fuss I made. I wasn't listening.'

Aarons chuckled. 'Never mind,' he said, 'I don't think you missed so much.'

'Michael,' she said, 'before we do anything else, do you mind if we just go back into the street for a few minutes?'

'No,' he said, 'but why?'

'Well I know it seems silly,' she said, 'but I've got a ladybird in my hand.'

Chapter Sixteen

The Reception

They deposited Elizabeth's ladybird on a bush in the churchyard opposite, and returned to the reception that was to follow the formal opening. The visitors had thronged to a further hall. There were the usual kinds of drink. The usual kinds of food. They found themselves on the edge of a group that was listening attentively to a tall, untidy young man with a moustache.

'The need is for bridges,' he was saying. 'Of course, we can't expect everyone in government and the civil service to be a scientist – that's impossible. Most simply lack the capacity. But at least everyone in responsible positions should be educated to the point where he can have some grasp of what scientists are saying. Some knowledge of the basic principles. We still don't even have that. Our schools aren't trying for it. The public doesn't understand it. Let someone find out that a kid's left school without reading Shakespeare, and fifty thousand old ladies are up in arms. But he can leave without the slightest knowledge of the second law of thermo-dynamics, and they couldn't care less.' He caught sight of Michael Aarons, and suddenly addressed him. 'Someone like you, I suppose, finds all this very difficult to follow?'

He was that kind of teacher who has learned to win easy laughter and a reputation for wit by that unpleasant game wherein a slow or ill-adjusted student is singled out for the amusement of others. A clergyman with a puzzled expression seemed made for such treatment, and, indeed, responded with entirely satisfactory confusion.

'Er – I'm sorry. Were you speaking to me?'

'You look as if you don't follow the argument,' said the young man in his best professional manner.

'Well – yes – I *was* wondering why the old ladies were so wrong.'

'The second law of thermo-dynamics states . . .' began the young man –

'Excuse me. I know what it states,' said Aarons. 'What I don't understand is why the ladies ought to think it's as important to know about heat not being able to pass from cold things to hot, as it is to know Shakespeare?'

The young man looked momentarily startled, but recovered.

'I'm glad to see a member of your profession so well-informed. As for your question – the answer is simple. In scientific terms, knowing about the second law of thermo-dynamics is equivalent to knowing about Shakespeare in cultural terms.'

'And you regard the two as equally important?'

'Certainly I do.'

Aarons nodded, and smiled politely. 'I see. Thank you.' He started to turn away.

'Do you disagree?'

Aarons turned back, and met his questioner's eye. 'Why yes, I think I do.'

The young man folded his arms, and gave a quick glance towards those round him. 'Why?' he asked.

'Well,' – Aarons hesitated for a second – 'if I had missed the second law of thermo-dynamics, I should have missed an important hypothesis. But Shakespeare?' He shook his head. 'If I had missed Shakespeare, I should have missed something of life itself. The two are not equivalent.'

The young man snorted. 'I imagined you'd say something like that,' he said, and turned away.

Aarons found himself facing a sea of hostile, amused, or

indifferent faces. At the same time, he felt a cool hand in his, and heard a familiar voice in his ear.

'Come on, you've smitten enough Philistines for one night. There's work to be done.'

'What?'

'Work,' said Elizabeth, towing him along. 'Come along. This way.'

'I don't understand. What are we doing?' asked the priest, as he found himself guided between double swing doors, and on to an area of open tarmac between the hall and another large building.

'Exploring,' said Elizabeth. 'Looking for evils, of course. What did you come here for?'

'But we can't just go wandering about the place as if we owned it.'

'Of course we can,' said Elizabeth. 'Just wander. Wander boldly. Didn't some clergyman say that? If anyone asks what we're doing, you just play the twitty vicar and leave the rest to Liz. Come on. Over here. Just stroll. Not a care in the world. Chin up. Perfect right to be here. That's right.'

In spite of himself, Aarons found himself strolling through an arch, and into a long quadrangle. It was evidently surrounded by the main laboratories and workshops, a mass of glass and aluminium that gleamed in the yellow sodium glare. Signs of recent construction were obvious. A heap of scaffolding. Several pieces of machinery. It was quiet, though, after the hubbub of the reception, and a light breeze was refreshing. They walked across freshly laid paving.

'A stream used to run under here,' said Elizabeth, 'but they've diverted it. Into the Thames. Higher up.'

'How on earth do you know that?' asked Aarons.

'Last week. The public library and our local paper. It's amazing what's public knowledge if you take the trouble to ask. Hang on. I copied out a plan.'

She produced from her handbag a piece of paper, and peered at it. Aarons was shattered.

'Now why on earth didn't I think of that?' he asked.

'I told you,' said Elizabeth, lining up her paper with the buildings, 'you're no good at spotting evils. It takes an expert. And I *am* married to a policeman! Ah – that's right. Through here. It ought to get really interesting. Come on!'

Chapter Seventeen

Hadrian's Grave

Elizabeth led the way confidently to a corner of the quadrangle, through a narrow space, and out onto a wide area. There were halls of residence on each side, and between, a chaos of rubble, building material, and tools. Fifty yards ahead of them, a high, barbed-wire fence. In front of that, a well-lit sign.

— D A N G E R —

THIS IS A HISTORIC SITE AND ITS PRESENT CONDITION IS EXTREMELY DANGEROUS
ABSOLUTELY NO ADMISSION UNDER ANY CIRCUMSTANCES
GUARD DOGS AND SECURITY MEN PATROL

'That,' she said, 'is Hadrian's Grave. It's what your young men were on about. I found out quite a lot from the library. Apparently it was called that in the sixteenth century. The book didn't know why, but didn't think it had anything to do with Hadrian. For a long time there was an inn here. There's a witticism in Boswell about 'making an end at the Grave' apparently. Seems an odd name for a pub, but there you are. The place had some connection with the Hellfire Club – though the book was a bit vague about that. Then it was burnt down, and afterwards there was a warehouse.' (She peered again at her notes.) 'Oh, yes. Someone found some Roman brickwork whilst they were building an extension in 1937. That's all. Come on. Let's stroll.'

They got within feet of the barbed wire. They had time to notice earthworks, and a dark entrance; but there was no obvious way in through the fence. Elizabeth was just about to suggest they walked along the fence to the left, when a voice hailed them.

‘Hi – you two! Where the hell d’you think you’re going?’

A figure emerged from the shadows in the direction in which they were moving. As it did so, the wind seemed to change direction for a few seconds, and Aarons noticed a strange, unpleasant smell.

‘Can’t you read?!’

Suddenly, and to Michael Aarons’ amazement, Elizabeth seemed to become a different person. She fluttered and flattered toward the advancing figure. She oozed good-natured incompetence.

‘Oh – *good* evening – we’re *so* glad to see you. We seem to have taken a wrong turning –’

‘Well, this is out of bounds.’

‘Oh, really? We *are* sorry, aren’t we, Vicar?’

‘Er –’

‘This is our Vicar. I’m afraid I was feeling a little faint, and he kindly brought me out for some air and we seem to have taken a wrong turning.’

‘At the reception, are you?’

‘Yes, that’s right. The Vicar’s *so* interested in education “Knowledge is the key to life”, he says, and –’

‘Well, the reception’s back through there.’

‘Oh, thank you *so* much. That *is* kind. And I’m feeling much better now, thank you. Come along, Vicar. *Good* night, then.’

‘Good night.’

The man did not sound as if he meant it, and gazed sullenly after them as they made their way back. ‘The Vicar appeared to be affected with some kind of twitch.

Elizabeth said nothing, until they were back in the car – then she grasped Aarons' arm.

'Michael – don't think me mad – but – do you remember what I told you about last November – about when they tried to kill me?'

'Yes. Of course I do.'

'Well – I really think there may be a connection between what happened then and that place – Hadrian's Grave.'

Michael Aarons waited for her to continue.

'Did you notice the smell? Just after that man started shouting?'

'I certainly did. Dreadful. Like rotten fish.'

'That's right. A sort of dead smell. Well – I'm sure it's the same. The same smell. It brought the whole thing back to me. What happened that night. I was so surprised I thought for a second I was going to faint again.'

'You hid it remarkably well.'

'Oh – the man was shouting and then we moved away and then we were busy.'

'*You* certainly were,' said Aarons. 'An amazing performance!'

'But for that second, Michael, I was sure. Absolutely sure. I've never smelt anything like it anywhere else in my life. Really.'

By the time they reached the Commercial Road, it was beginning to rain.

'Incidentally,' said Elizabeth as they drove past St Paul's Cathedral, 'well done with the Philistine!'

'Philistine?' said Aarons, whose mind was on the evening before them.

'Thermo-dynamics and all that!'

'Oh!' Aarons shook his head. 'I'm not too proud of that.'

'Why?' asked Elizabeth.

'That young man. I was very hard on him. I didn't do justice to his case. For some people there *is* life – even inspiration – in a scientific hypothesis. I didn't grant him that.'

'Now Michael, stop apologizing!' said Elizabeth, who did not gladly suffer attacks on her friends. 'He was on his own ground and he was jolly rude. Serve him right!'

Chapter Eighteen

The Council of War

They had been back at St Andrew's for about half an hour – time to drink coffee, to eat a little of the supper Michael Aarons had provided, and to tell David the latest news – when the doorbell rang. Michael Aarons answered it. It was Charlie. Introductions were made, and the duties of hospitality fulfilled. Splodger took to Charlie Brown at once, prancing round him in delight and then, when he sat down, curling at his feet.

'It's because she heard you were a professor in the University,' said Elizabeth. 'She has intellectual pretensions, you know!'

Charlie laughed. The council began.

At Michael Aarons' request, they started by telling their stories. He, David and Elizabeth told Charlie all that they knew or could guess of the events of the previous All Hallows' Eve. Then Charlie told his story of the observations at Siding Spring, of their likely significance, of his dream, and of his meeting with Michael Aarons.

At the end of Charlie's recital there was silence. David found himself oddly nonplussed. Almost, detached. It was all so absurdly simple. If they were really to believe this quiet young man who spoke (he had to admit it) with such authority, then they, and everyone else, probably had about ten days to live. The policeman in him appreciated perhaps better than Charlie the real nature of the diplomats' dilemma. He could picture only too vividly the scenes of chaos that would follow, when the world knew.

In the mean time, *he* knew. And what of it? What about all

that worrying about his job? And his future? What about the arrival of Sproglet? It was all an illusion. There would be no future for any of them. Not for him. Or Elizabeth. Or Sproglet. None of them.

He looked at the solidarity of Michael Aarons' furniture. At the carpet. At Splodger, pretending to be asleep. A fragment of an old Tom Lehrer song came into his mind:

'Oh, we'll all go together when we go,
All suffused with an incandescent glow – '

and he smiled wryly. Marvellous. Armageddon. And all he could do was remember a joke about it. Odd. Odd, really, how little he felt. At least for the moment. Maybe more feeling would come later. But for the present, now that he came to think about it, he really felt nothing. Charlie Brown might as well have told them it was going to rain. Of course, it couldn't last. The feelings *would* come later. With realization. When it sunk in, as his mother would have said. But for the present there was nothing. Or very little.

And what about Elizabeth? He looked across at her, and at once felt electricity.

Elizabeth was angry. If she had been asked, With whom?, and had had time and inclination to think clearly, she would probably have answered, With the universe, or, With God. The universe had, after all, just given her the promise of Sproglet. And now the universe proposed that Sproglet should have no more being than Sproglet had already. What sort of a trick was that? As it was, her outrage exploded in an angry challenge to the most authoritative figure (for her) in the room.

'Michael – why have we been told all this? Why have you got us here? What's the point of it?'

'Because we prefer truth to illusions,' replied Aarons bluntly. 'And because there's something here that links to you – to what happened on All Saints' Eve. You were angry then because you felt you had been made into a victim. Do you want to give up now? Do you want *just* to be a victim?'

Elizabeth was still angry, but her voice was calmer. 'All right,' she said. 'What link?'

The priest paused, and gathered his thoughts before replying. Then –

'I admit, I'm not exactly sure,' he said. 'But two things make me think that there must be a connection. First – there's the coincidence of dates. The Ceremony on All Saints' Eve, and the phenomenon seen by Charlie and his colleagues only a few hours later. Next – and it was some time before this occurred to me – the exact match between what I imagine to be the object of the Ceremony, and what Charlie thinks may actually be happening.'

Again, the priest hesitated. Clearly, even to talk about the *Beriyt et-Mavet* made him uncomfortable.

'The point is this. The Ceremony of the *Beriyt et-Mavet* is intended to destroy. It's an assault upon creation itself. Its centre, God forgive us, is a formal and considered reversal of the divine Name. If such an intention were coupled with real power, and not directed to any particular end, but just generally, then what Charlie describes is exactly what we might expect. A threat of total destruction.'

'But David stopped the ceremony,' said Elizabeth.

'Yes. I suppose the question is – did I stop it, or did I only interrupt it?' said David quietly.

'If the ceremony had been completed, wouldn't it have – got me?' said Elizabeth.

Aarons considered the question.

'It was James Darrell only, I think, who pledged your life. And he died, as I recall, at 6.50 a.m.'

David nodded.

'Well then. His life for yours. From the moment of his death, you would no longer be involved. But suppose someone else completed the ceremony soon after Darrell died? According to Charlie, the phenomenon was first noted at 12.20 a.m. Greenwich Mean Time on that morning,' – he paused, and looked at Charlie, who also nodded – 'which leaves nearly four hours for someone to have done it – after Darrell's death, and before the sighting.'

'And you really think that a ceremony carried on that morning might have led to this – star?'

'I only say – there *seems* to be a connection. Of timing. And of purpose.'

'There's also a difficulty,' said David.

The others looked at him.

'Michael – I admit your time-scheme fits like a glove – from where *we* are. But if I follow Charlie correctly, this explosion actually happened thirty thousand years ago. It's only its *results* that first appeared to us on November first. So how can something someone did in London on that day have an effect on something that happened thirty thousand years ago?'

'I think I can answer that,' said Charlie. 'At least – I can mathematically.'

The others looked at him.

'It's to do with dimensions,' he said, taking a notebook and pencil out of his pocket and starting to draw. 'The dimensions in which we operate. Just imagine for one minute that you were confined to two dimensions – a flat surface:

Now, to get from A to B you would obviously have to go a certain distance – let's say (since we don't know the scale of my drawing) quite a long way. Now – imagine the surface curved (as space is, incidentally):

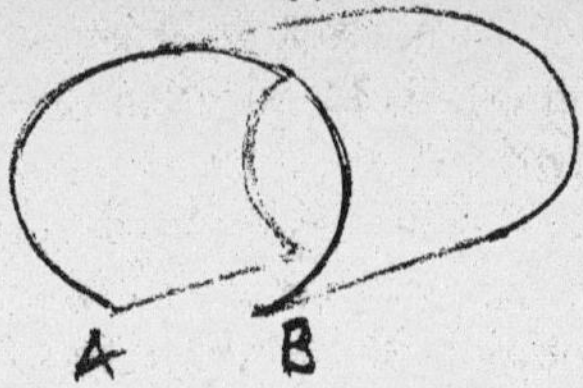

So long, of course, as you were still confined to two dimensions, you would have to go the distance from A to B that we already noted. But now imagine that you learnt a way to get out of two dimensions into the third dimension. You could then go by a very brief journey from A to B – like this:

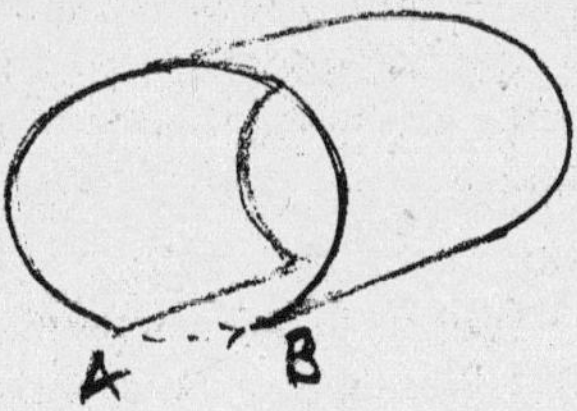

Do you see?'

'Yes. So far.' said David.

The others nodded.

'Well now. We normally operate in four dimensions – three dimensions of space, and time. Mathematically, however, it's quite possible to envisage a fifth, though of course we don't know how to reach it. But suppose that some immense spiritual – or counter-spiritual – force is unleashed. Perhaps it's precisely through the fifth dimension that it operates. In which case it's perfectly possible to see how a prayer now – or a curse – might effect something thirty thousand light years distant – like a fly crossing from one edge of our paper to the other. Do you see?'

'Yes,' said David, 'I actually think I do.'

'Of course,' said Charlie, 'it's sheer speculation. I'm not actually claiming that it's what *is* happening. I'm only saying that mathematically it's perfectly possible.'

'Isn't there something like it in one of Charles Williams' books?' said David slowly – 'about a girl in the twentieth century who helps her ancestor – a reformation martyr?'

'Yes!' said Charlie, '*Descent into Hell* – that's the one. Naturally, he doesn't talk about the maths: but he certainly saw how the idea could work.'

'The Law of Exchange,' said Aarons softly.

'Hadrian's Grave!' exclaimed Elizabeth, breaking everyone's train of thought.

'What?' said Charlie.

'Hadrian's Grave – the archaeological site at Cranston College. You've shown us the thing is possible. And Hadrian's Grave has to be the place where they did it – finished the ceremony.'

The others looked at her.

'Think! They couldn't have done it at the Academy because of the fire. There would have been firemen leaping all over it. But they did have time to get to Cranston College. And we know they already had a connection with it. David spotted that in his inquiries last year. What's more, it's the right *sort* of place.'

'How?' asked David.

'It's ancient. And in the past it's had some connection with evil. Michael knows. I looked it up. Wouldn't that be the sort of place they'd use?'

'Yes,' said Michael Aarons, 'I think it would. And then, of course, you noticed the smell.'

'Exactly!' said Elizabeth. 'The same smell as the night they tried to kill me. Abominable. I'd recognize it anywhere. And it's there. It has to be the place.'

'It certainly seems likely,' said Michael Aarons. 'Does anyone have any other suggestions?'

No one had.

'So,' said David, 'what? I take it you didn't just ask us here so we could come up with a brilliant theory. Do you think there's something we should do?'

Chapter Nineteen

The Resolution

There was a pause.

'If that place has been claimed for the Destroyer,' said Michael Aarons, 'then my instinct is that someone should go quickly and deny that claim. An exorcism would be proper, but it would take time to arrange. Just to go and pray would be something. But if that claim has been made, it should be challenged.'

'Yes,' said Elizabeth slowly, 'and if all times are in some way accessible, then maybe . . .' she hesitated, seeking a way to articulate her thought.

' – all times are redeemable?' suggested Aarons, with a mental apology to the poet.

'Yes!' said Elizabeth. 'Exactly!'

'Are you saying that doing this might change something?' asked David. 'I mean – about the star?'

'I don't know,' said Aarons. 'Perhaps. Or perhaps all it will mean is that when death comes, someone will have taken a stand on the side of life. I don't know. But I think we should do what we can.'

'I'm sure I must go,' said Charlie quietly. 'It all fits. The dream. The church. You. I've got to.'

'If you feel like that,' said Aarons, 'then I certainly think you must – '

'There!' Charlie's spectacles almost fell off as he jerked to his feet in excitement. 'That's exactly what you said in my dream. "You must!" '

'Well,' said Michael Aarons, 'but I was going to say – your dream involves me too. Unless you have an absolute conviction that you must go alone, I think perhaps I should come with you. I have some experience in these matters, and that may be useful.'

Charlie sighed. 'Actually, I'd like that very much. I'm completely out of my depth.'

'Good. Then that is decided. I will come.'

'In which case,' said David, who had wandered over to the window, 'it looks as though we are in for a soaking.'

' "We"?' said Aarons.

'Well, you both seem bent on it. I don't see how I can let you go blundering about in the dark performing acts of goodwill or whatever by yourselves. You need someone, even if it's only to hold a torch.'

'Yes,' said Aarons. 'We also need all the goodwill – and faith – we can get.'

'I'll go and put my jeans on,' said Elizabeth.

'Hey – is this a place for you?' said David, 'Especially now?'

'Come off it, darling,' said Elizabeth. 'If Charlie's right, none of us, including Sproglet, has a lot of future – unless something changes. Michael just said you needed all the goodwill you can get.'

Aarons' face was grim. 'Yes,' he said quietly, 'we do.'

David grimaced. 'All right,' he said at last, 'I suppose I can't argue with that. What exactly are you going to do, then?'

'I imagine the first problem,' said Aarons, 'is to get in at all.'

'Well actually,' said Charlie with a wry grin, 'the place *is* supposed to be in association with London University, and I *am* on the faculty. I suppose I could say I thought I had a right to wander in with my friends and look round if I wanted to.'

David smiled. 'Not bad,' he said. 'I've been given cover stories that were worse. And with luck you won't have to use it. Judging by what I've seen of higher education security, we walk in looking as if we knew where we were going, and nobody will take the slightest notice.'

'They were actually quite strict with us tonight,' said Elizabeth.

'That's because they had the Minister and the Mayor and God-knows-who there. In fact – there'll probably never be a better time to walk in than the next hour or so. After getting rid of all those VIP's without disaster, even if they do have any security, ten to one it'll be sprawling about congratulating itself.'

'Then that sounds hopeful,' said Aarons. 'But let us be quite clear – if what we've speculated is correct, after that we're up against something very dangerous indeed. If we go in God's name, intending as best we can to serve God, then certainly nothing can harm us eternally. But physically – that's a different matter.' He looked at Charlie. 'You've claimed a chief part in this, and in view of what brought you here, I cannot deny your claim. I'd be less than honest if I suppressed my conviction that he who bears the greatest part will bear the greatest danger.'

Charlie Brown nodded.

Aarons looked at his watch. 'It is nine twenty-five. If anyone needs me, I shall be in church for the next thirty minutes. I suggest we assemble in the hall at ten, make our final preparations, and go.'

The others nodded.

'May I use your study?' asked Charlie. 'I want to write something.'

'Of course,' said Michael Aarons.

David and Elizabeth were walking towards the door, when suddenly Elizabeth turned and went back to Aarons, who was still by the fire.

'Sorry!' she said, 'for being ratty!' – and kissed him.

He looked at her and smiled. 'Bless you!' he said. 'You

and I don't have to apologize for things like that.'

'I know. But there it is – anyway!'

Hand in hand, David and Elizabeth went to their room. Splodger trotted behind them.

David was grinning.

'I thought love meant not having to say you were sorry,' he observed.

'That's the biggest load of balderdash I've ever heard,' she replied.

He chuckled.

Across the passage, the study door creaked as Charlie closed it.

The house grew silent.

The speculations of Michael Aarons and his friends were remarkably close to the truth. It was, in fact, the Chairman of the Academy for Philosophical Studies, horribly burned and dying, who had escaped from the Academy on the night of the fire. He had dragged himself several miles across London to the ancient site under Cranston College which had been known in the eighteenth century as Hadrian's Grave. Centuries before, Hadrian's Grave had actually been a temple of Mithras, the Lightbringer, dedicated by Roman legionaries to the highest symbol of truth and justice that they knew. It had long since been desecrated, and placed instead under the domain of darkness. Here the Chairman of the Academy had come and, with his dying breath, invoked the Darkness. Here he had completed the terrible ritual of the Cōvenant with Death, consecrating all with the offering of his own life.

Darkness had answered and now, at the heart of the ancient site, there was an evil: a corrupt spirituality of vast authority. The citizens of East London, the faculty and students of Cranston College, even the police officers who visited the site – they did not see the evil. Nor did they recognize its influence. But they were affected by it, just the same. Vibrations of its joyless vigil ran along power cables and gas mains, phone lines and water pipes, seeping negation into earth and air. Hence a thousand local manifestations of disorder extended (had one traced them on a map) a mile or so outward in each direction from the centre. Failed telephones and broken traffic lights. Inexplicable power failures and outbursts of criminal malice. These were the signs of its presence and the echoes of its being.

They offered, however, no clue to its purpose. It had been invoked as Destroyer: so it now lay, waiting the advent of a destruction that it had itself invoked from the heart of the galaxy. This destruction would affect the totality of the Earth, so being the proper fulfilment and answer to the Ritual of the Covenant with Death.

This was what lay at the heart of Cranston College. This was what waited for those who now chose to challenge its dominion.

Chapter Twenty

Regrets

Charlie Brown sat at Aaron's desk.

He had warmed quickly to David and Elizabeth, to say nothing of their beautiful dog; and he already liked and trusted Michael Aarons. So the three of them had stimulated him through the conference. But with the stimulus of their presence gone, he found himself depressed and afraid. He thought of Jacquie, and it suddenly occurred to him that in the last couple of weeks and especially in the last couple of days, he had been acting like an idiot. Maybe the pressure he was under from this other business was part of the reason, but the fact remained, he had been an idiot. And an insensitive idiot at that. What had he cared when she said she had to be with her mother? Had it occurred to him that the loyalty and compassion she was showing her mother was the quality he valued most in her? And then – in response to his 'offer' of 'freedom' (as if she were not free anyway) – when she had said so beautifully, 'All I want is to be with you' – how had he responded? He had gone babbling on about his concerns and his view of their relationship, as if she had no mind in the matter at all.

There was a scratch at the door, twice repeated. Curious, he went and opened it. Splodger stood looking at him until he invited her in, then she walked to the desk, and sat herself by his chair. Having seen that her master and mistress were well, it was natural for her to seek the most troubled person in the house. Charlie did not know this, but he was grateful for her company. He sat again at the desk, caressing her head.

The fact was, he wanted Jacquie so much, he had almost stopped caring about her: becoming totally absorbed in his own supposings. What would he give to have that conversation over again! To be at the moment when she said, 'All I want is to be with you' – so that he could tell her what that meant to him.

Well. What to write? Look at the time! In just a few minutes, what to write? He must try. He picked up the pen, and scribbled. Then glanced through it.

'Little enough. But it'll have to do.'

He wrote a second note to his mother.

'Lord,' he thought, as he looked at the two envelopes, 'I don't deserve the people you've put in my life. I really don't.'

He tidied the envelopes into the centre of the desk, got up, and went to the door. Michael Aarons was just coming up the stairs.

'Michael,' he said, 'is that you? I'm ready.'

'Well done,' said the priest. 'Then so am I.'

For a moment they stood together on the landing.

'Why me?' asked Charlie suddenly.

'I don't know,' replied the priest. 'I don't expect it's for any reason you'd find very flattering.

'I feel pathetic.'

'Who doesn't?' said the priest. 'You have goodwill. A measure of faith. You are trying to be obedient. You may have more power than you think. And, of course, you're in love.'

'I've made a pretty fair mess of that,' said Charlie.

'Who hasn't?' said Aarons. 'It's still a gift.'

'Michael – there's just one thing. On the desk. A couple of envelopes. They're addressed. One's for Jacquie. The other's for my mother. If anything happens to me, and you come out of it – could you try to see they get them? And explain what happened?'

Michael Aarons nodded.
'Yes,' he said. 'Of course.'

Chapter Twenty-One

Return to Hadrian's Grave

At ten o'clock, Michael Aarons appeared at the top of the stairs. He was carrying a small, battered leather case. David and Elizabeth were in the hall, talking softly. They had assembled torches, wellington boots, and a piece of rope. Elizabeth looked curiously at Aarons' case. She had seen it many times before in his study at Salisbury in the days when he was her parish priest. She knew that it contained the vessels with which he celebrated Holy Communion for the sick.

'Communion?' she said.

'Quite right,' he replied. 'I thought it possible we might decide to have a celebration. What better way to reverse the *Beriyt et-Mavet?*' For a moment, the Archdeacon in him surfaced. 'As it's someone else's parish, I ought to have the incumbent's permission, really.' He smiled. 'But he's a good fellow. He'll forgive me.'

'Whose car?' asked David.

'Mine, I think,' said Aarons. It was an estate, so they could put their pieces of equipment in the back. 'But perhaps you would drive?'

'If you like,' said David.

'Right,' said Aarons, 'then let's remind ourselves that we are in God's hands.'

The small group gathered round the priest.

They left the house a few minutes later. It was now raining heavily. All of them were preoccupied, and when David went back to the house for an extra torch, it was perhaps not surprising that no one noticed Splodger, who slipped through the open front door, scuttled across shining gravel to the tail-gate, and climbed discreetly in. When David came back with the torch and dumped it on top of the wellingtons and rope, even then he did not see her, curled in a dark patch beside the spare wheel. But then, she knew perfectly well that she had been told to 'stay', and on such occasions, was remarkably skilled in the art of making herself small.

David slammed the rear shut. A few minutes later, they were off.

The rain was a help. It is a good deal easier not to draw attention to torches and a coil of rope if you can hide them under a bulky raincoat than if you are more lightly clad. David's estimate of what would happen when they went into the college proved entirely accurate. The whole reception area had an odd, after-the-party air. Most people had left, but there were still enough about – a group talking noisily in a corner, a couple of students discussing earnestly on a seat beside a large palm – to make their own entry comparatively inconspicuous. Aarons attracted most attention, for priests were not common in that place, but he was engaged in conversation with Charlie, who looked exactly like what he was – a University lecturer – and although a couple of pairs of eyes looked up, no real notice was taken, even of him. David gazed curiously about. Like Elizabeth, he found himself reminded of Gatwick Airport. With maybe a touch of the new Euston Station. Elizabeth wondered if all the plants were plastic. Had she not been so anxious to avoid drawing attention to herself, she would have gone and looked.

They walked through passages, and then splashed across the quadrangles which Aarons and Elizabeth had already visited that evening. Rounding the last corner, they could see the brightly-lit fence that surrounded Hadrian's Grave, and along to the left, a stoutly-built watchman's hut by the entrance. The lights at that end of the fence must for some reason have been off when Aarons and Elizabeth visited earlier, or they could not have failed to see it. Not only was it now visible: there was a light inside, and the head of the occupant could be seen.

They sheltered in a doorway, out of sight of the hut.

'Problem!' said Elizabeth. 'What do we do?'

'I could try to talk my way in,' suggested Charlie.

'Hang on,' said David. 'Let's save that for desperation.' He felt in his pocket. 'Has anyone got a ten-penny piece?'

'Yes, here!' said Michael Aarons. 'What are you going to do?'

'Don't ask!' said David, and went back the way they had come.

Several minutes passed. Then, to their surprise, the door to the hut opened, and the watchman left. Mackintosh collar turned up against the driving rain, he walked by without noticing them, and on towards the main building. Another minute passed, and David re-appeared.

'He's gone!' said Elizabeth.

'I know,' said David with a grin. 'Wonderful things, telephones. See the cable – they've even put one in the watchman's hut. Very sensible.'

'David – you didn't!'

'Come on,' said David. 'I see they don't have a watchman in that hut, so obviously they don't mind people looking round. Let's go, shall we?'

They splashed and scampered to the entrance, then followed a path inside the fence, to the right. They had to make their way alongside the mound, and the going was not easy. The ground sloped sharply towards the barbed wire, and the way was no doubt slippery at best. Soaked, it was a nightmare. The rain was now falling in sheets, and it was hard to see anything at all. 'Oh, Sproglet,' muttered

Elizabeth through clenched teeth, 'maybe we should have taken David's advice and stayed at home!' But she clung to her torch and blundered on.

Suddenly the entrance to the mound was there. They plunged into cloaking shadow. It was good, for a moment, simply to be out of the din and the drenching. Then, as Elizabeth's senses adjusted, she recognized something that the rain had shielded from her. The smell. Again that extraordinary, unpleasant smell.

'Along here,' said David softly. 'It seems to go along here. Phew! What a smell!'

They switched on torches. The passage turned left, then very slightly upwards, then right again, and down steep steps. Around them, stonework and darkness. The silence was restful, but a little ominous. The steps went down for ten feet or so, and at the bottom they found themselves in what appeared, in the light of the torches, to be a plain square chamber that could have held a hundred people. Good stonework. Several pieces of stone lying about. Gravelly floor. Exactly, David reflected, as the police had described it. They flashed their torches about. There were no other exits. There was nothing to remark on. Save that unpleasant smell. And somewhere, the slow drip of water on stone. It was almost, after all that had led up to it, an anti-climax.

'Well,' said Aarons, 'we are here.'

A pause.

'I don't think this is it,' said Elizabeth at last.

'Where else can we go?' said David.

'I don't know,' she replied. 'I just don't think this is it. There's nothing here.'

'What do you think?' asked Aarons, turning to Charlie.

'I agree with Elizabeth,' said Charlie. 'There's nothing here.'

'Then we must look for another way out.'

It was David who spotted it. A square of stone that seemed slightly different from the others – that seemed to give when he touched it.

'Here – what's this? I think I've found something.'

The others crowded round him. He pressed again. At first nothing happened. He slid his hand to the right, and pressed once more. The wall groaned, and a section of it began to swing back. It moved until it stood at an angle of forty-five degrees to its original position. Opened beside it was a dark, narrow entrance.

Chapter Twenty-Two

The Meeting

'Wait!' said David, as they surged forward. 'We don't want any nasty accidents. Can you give me a hand?'

With Charlie's and Michael Aarons' help he manhandled a piece of stone until it was so placed that the entrance could not close by accident. Then he took from his pocket a box of matches, struck one, and held it into the tunnel. It burned strongly, flickering slightly as in a draught. He lit another, and walked a few yards in. It continued to burn with the same slight flicker.

'All right. Let's try it.'

In single file, with David leading, they crossed the threshold.

Within seconds, they seemed to have passed a barrier. The stonework on each side of them looked and felt immeasurably older than that they had left. Instead of large, well-squared blocks, small rougher pieces were set in thick mortar. A few inches above the floor, their torches picked up a line of red, though whether it was for decoration or some other purpose, they did not know. At one point there was a stone slab set in the wall. It bore an inscription, but was badly worn. They could make out two words, and part of a third:

DIVVS MITHRAS VEN . . .

' "Divine Mithras comes – or came",' whispered Elizabeth. 'Is that what it says?'

Aarons nodded. 'Yes. We know there was *one* temple of Mithras in London. Why not another? It would be the sort of place they would choose.'

'Look! Further on!' said David, shining the torch.

There was a second slab, again much worn. Most of it was beyond deciphering, but one line stood out –

ET NOS SERVASTI ETERNALI SANGVINE FVSO

' "And you have saved us by shedding eternal blood"? That sounds Christian,' said Elizabeth.

Aarons shook his head. 'I think not. I think it meant Mithras slaying the bull,' he said. 'But never mind! – perhaps we should take the writers to have said better than they knew.'

'I think we're near,' said Charlie. 'We must go.'

He spoke with authority. The others did not argue.

The way was narrow, curving left, and slightly downwards. With each step they seemed to move backwards in time, decade by decade into the past. Suddenly David held up his hand and halted. The others halted too. His reason at once became apparent. The stench, to which Elizabeth had begun to grow accustomed, trebled in strength. She was nauseated. Later, she remembered leaning against a damp wall, and seeing the silhouetted figures of the other three ahead of her – Michael Aarons and Charlie Brown against the opposite wall, David on the same side as herself. She struggled to reach him, and called his name. Despite mounting nausea, he heard her. With one last effort he turned, caught her hand, and pulled her to him. He could do no more. Helpless, they lay together against the rough stone.

Then came the scream.

It must be described as a scream, since at least that word speaks of agony and intensity. But by no means does that alone describe what came to them out of the darkness – a piercing something that went through brain and heart and pulled them inexorably forward. They were staggering, as if wrenched by a gale. Hair, hands, bodies were disintegrating. They lost each other. Then, blackness.

For some time now, Charlie had known. Back in the large chamber, for a moment he had hoped that it might be foolishness, though his instincts told him otherwise. With David's discovery, that hope had fled. He knew again the fear – the fear he had known in his Dream. There was a cup to drink, and it was his. Precisely what, or what kind of horror they approached, or what there was for him to do – this he neither guessed nor wondered; but that there was horror and that there was a task – this he no longer doubted.

Not at all, in his striving, did he notice something that walked softly at his side. A hint of white. He only knew he must go forward. Then came the scream. Lost and blinded, he fell.

They felt gravel beneath them, but could see and hear nothing. Not 'see nothing' in the normal sense of that phrase – but literally nothing. Absolutely nothing. David put his hands to his eyes and moved them inches away and it made no difference. Only a blackness so deep it seemed to deny even the possibility of light. Elizabeth drew breath to cry out, and choked. Yet her choking made no sound, and when she tried to shout, she felt her lips move as in a dream, but heard nothing. She knew that David was near, but she could not find him.

A gleam of white. They saw what Charlie had not seen. The gleam turned to silver and into their vision came – the wolf. She was silver. Not white, but silver – gleaming from within with a pale, cool light. Around her, total blackness. Yet the wolf seemed unafraid and unconfused. Where there was neither dimension nor solidarity, she gave her own. In the instant of seeing her, David and Elizabeth found and clasped each other's hands. But still, unable to see each other, they watched the wolf. They had no idea of her size, for there was no way to relate her to anything. Only they retained an impression of joyful, animal strength, an ardent power. The wolf jumped, as if to a higher level, sat, as if on a flat surface, and looked about. In one way, she seemed familiar. And yet they had certainly never looked on such a creature before. She was a beast from Eden. A beast from Paradise, when the world was young.

The wolf yawned. Then, with a jerk of attention, like a dog called by a well-loved human, turned, seemed to jump down, and trotted to a place on their left. She stooped, and bent her head. In the faint glow, they saw the face and form of Charlie Brown, unconscious. The wolf was licking his face. Charlie blinked, and shook his head, touched the wolf, and said something they could not hear. Then, slowly, he got to his feet.

Chapter Twenty-Three

The Battle

Whether there was now light around them, or whether there had been light all the time and their eyes had not adjusted to it, or whether, indeed, they saw at all, they could never be sure. But by some means they were all now able to distinguish each other as well as Charlie who stood, tall and still, his hand on the head of the wolf, and faced the darkness.

Out of the darkness, a voice. Or, rather, the denial of voice. A whisper of evil.

'*How dare you come to disturb us*?'

The wolf growled. The darkness seemed, as they watched, to grow – pulsating, summoning, claiming – the infinite void. And as it grew, so did their awareness of Charlie and the beast. It *was* Charlie – they were never in any doubt of that – but he seemed taller than they had known.

He spoke, and in his voice compassion and a grief older than the foundation of the world.

'This is not your place, friend. You should not be here.'

The pulsating darkness wavered. For a long second there was hesitancy – then the pulsation renewed, and the blackness grew – and with it the whisper, the soft echo of a festering malignancy.

'*You shall be destroyed*.'

Charlie spoke again:

'Where are our children?'

'*Doomed*.'

Like an evil drumbeat it came upon them. The darkness

lapped forward, then flared in a sudden blast that must surely engulf them.

But through the blast, beyond the rage and the danger, Charlie Brown saw something else – though why the insight came to him, and by what power he was able to act upon it, he did not know.

Loneliness.

The creature was lonely.

His enemy, the enemy of the human race, was solitary.

Whatever its history – a billion years of negation – the reward of that history was to be alone.

Without hope.

And now, Charlie saw himself. Infinitely lower in the scale of creation than the fallen archon he faced – yet possessed of a capacity at that moment powerful. Compassion. That single searing movement of love by which the Eternal had been bound to a decaying creation at Bethlehem and on Calvary, assuming it, that it might be redeemed.

And now? Charlie Brown – the finger tip of divine glory? What if he refused? Had God no other means? Infinite means, of course. Another Bethlehem. A deeper Calvary. 'Have I not many words for many worlds?' But what now of Charlie Brown? He could abandon the creature. He could withdraw. Back behind Michael Aarons and the others. Back to the beginning of the tunnel. Back to the streets of London. The underground. The airport. New York. And Jacquie. 'Hi, princess!' All it needed was one decisive act. An act of which he was, in one sense, perfectly capable. He must abandon the creature.

He could not.

Why had Jacquie stayed with her mother when she wanted to be with Charlie? Why had she helped the woman with the child by the East Battery? Simply because she obeyed a quality in herself that was, for him, the chief part of her glory. And if he went to her now, abandoning the creature, his going and their union would be founded on the betrayal of that quality. The decisive act required of him was an act that denied everything he saw in her. It was an act of cruelty.

So, to be loyal to Jacquie, he must refuse Jacquie. He must choose the creature.

He must refuse Jacquie.

At the formation of the thought, he groaned.

'God help me,' he said softly.

The warm, strong body of the wolf pressed against his thigh.

For a moment he trembled.

Then he grew still, looked at the thing before him, and spoke its name.

From the depths of a rejection older than time, the creature had known itself approached. Something disturbed it. Something challenged its hitherto impenetrable denial. For a moment its fixed attention to a perception of ancient wrong wavered. No human word or experience could comprehend what was threatened, for no human word or experience could comprehend its lostness. Asmodeus reared to destroy . . . and yet – some not-quite-smothered shred of a billion-year-old circuit flickered. Rejection sought, as ever, to support rejection by feeding upon rejection: and reaching, found not enough. So balked, Asmodeus hesitated. It was not emotion that disturbed it, for the creature was never created for passion: intelligence was its destiny – sheer intellectual charity as remote from human experience as the theology of Anselm from the ecstasy of a butterfly. Now a remote survival of that intelligence glimmered, raising the momentary possibility of attention to something other than its own injustice – the possibility, and the infinitely incalculable risk.

Before it stood the biped: disgusting combination of spirituality and matter. Yet from the biped – something. Its mouth moved. It uttered words. In themselves all words were to be rejected: for all words, however fatuous or malicious, held by their nature some echo of the Word to which, even now, Asmodeus must concede the being that Asmodeus denied with every atom of the being – that Asmodeus denied. Yet fatuity or malice – the denial of intelligence or the denial of charity – could, even through words, have offered Asmodeus the peculiar strength that Asmodeus sought. Instead, there was something else. Something that afforded Asmodeus no handle that could be grasped, no rage or rejection that could be absorbed. Even more dangerous, through the words there came, though faintly, the echo of an echo of a call that Asmodeus had heard at the dawn of creation. Certainly, it was merely the remotest foster-child of the great-great-granddaughter of that Voice. Yet still, there was something. For an instant, the strain ran true.

'Ashmodai! Come!'

Asmodeus, poised ready to destroy, hesitated. And in hesitating, was found.

As Charlie called the creature to himself, it seemed to him that they fell. Locked together, they fluttered in a void.

All the treacheries, all the petty cowardices and betrayals of his own life came before him. Between him and the creature lay only the question of degree. Both had betrayed. Betraying in particular, they had betrayed the universe. Betraying the universe, they had betrayed each other. They were lost.

It seemed, after a thousand years, that they sank to the final pit of negation. There was Nothing. And would be.

Suddenly, in that moment, they were held – by the One who had created them, and who now forgave, assuming their debt and its cost. In acquiring forgiveness of the One, Charlie acquired forgiveness of creation; forgiveness of the creature. And in being forgiven, forgave.

A devastating silence.

The creature had vanished. Yet in the instant before the silence, it seemed to the others that they heard: a single chord, the restoration of an ancient harmony. For one moment, they saw: the creature transformed, Archon of the Lord of Hosts: and they could have worshipped, save for a voice in the harmony that sang, 'I also am a servant. Worship God!' Their spirits soared. The silver wolf leapt and played, bouncing for joy, first around Charlie, then round them all. And Michael Aarons knew it was time. Book, chalice and paten lay before him. Quietly, he began.

It was such a liturgy as surpassed all their memories. Never could they speak precisely of what happened – not because it was confused, but because its order was too perfect; not because they were lost but because they, like the creature, were found.

Chapter Twenty-Four

The Liturgy

They heard a voice:

Arise, shine, for your light has come,
and the glory of the Lord has risen upon you –

and another that spoke with infinite understanding of the world's sorrow,

for behold, darkness shall cover the earth,
and thick darkness the peoples

and another that replied,

but the Lord will rise upon you,
and his glory will be seen

and then a symphonic crash, and they themselves were part of an impassioned cry:

Nations shall come to your light,
and Kings to the brightness of your rising!

Now it was quiet, almost homely; and the voice was very near –

the Word was made flesh,
and dwelt among us,
full of grace and truth;
we have beheld his glory.

The Peace was a dance and an exchange of laughter, whilst the wolf, their jester and playfellow, romped in the midst. Then they and the dance were swept to the altar, in a declaration of the first reality –

all things come of you,
and of your own have we given you.

There was ritual salutation, the demand and acknowledgement of joy, recital of the acts of creation and redemption – and the universe sang in uncounted tongues

Holy, Holy, Holy,
Sanctus, Sanctus, Sanctus,
Hagios, Hagios, Hagios,
Kadosh, Kadosh, Kadosh!

Then the voice of Michael Aarons again, reciting the tradition –

'. . . *Who in the same night that he was betrayed,*
took bread and gave you thanks . . . '

They ate and drank, and gave thanks for the coming of light. The priest dismissed them. With his dismissal he gave them blessing, and in that word it seemed that the ground leapt, solid earth danced, and the walls tumbled to their foundations. The roof was gone, great bars of golden light shining through the dust, whilst they themselves were swept through the uproar like music, and caught into light. For one moment it seemed they glimpsed the outskirts of the glory. They saw, and did not see. Silence.

Only Charlie heard a voice that summoned him further –

'Come!'

And suddenly before his eyes were spread the planets and stars he loved and, in his own way, served. The earth. The solar system. The Milky Way itself, a blazing disc with, at its centre, something like a sound misplaced, a candle lit before its time – and there came a voice, a breath, and the sound was taken into harmony, the flame flickered and withdrew to its own place. And still the vision grew. Other galaxies, and others. The Magellanic cloud. M31 in Andromeda. M81 in Ursa Major. And others and others. The cosmos itself, a single beloved jewel, a precious adornment, in the dance before the throne.

And again the voice said, 'Come!'

He felt warm air on his cheeks and heard gentle sea-swell and the cry of a bird. Jacquie was a few yards from him, standing on the Charleston Battery, looking out to sea, light breeze ruffling her hair. He sensed her sadness, and knew why she grieved. He saw in her hand a letter, and knew what it contained.

'Princess,' he said softly, and stood behind her, one hand on her shoulder, the other closing over hers as it lay on the rail. He touched the cloth of her dress and the coolness of her skin and felt the soft freshness of her hair. And as he stood, he felt warmth and strength and compassion, flowing into her through him from the One he served. She turned and looked into his eyes and so, for a moment, knew him. Then she was gone.

'She too shall be well,' said the voice, 'and all things shall be well.'

There was a host, such as none could number; a throne, and one that sat thereon, before whose face the heavens fled. Yet Charlie Brown, a thing of flesh and blood and earth, could stand erect in that presence, and lift his eyes, and speak in a tongue that until then he had not known was his. No earthly language could match those syllables, for they are of the archetype, the source and origin of all language. Only faintly may translation catch at the echo of their joy – 'My Mother and my Father, my Saviour and my Sovereign, my Lord and my God!'

Elizabeth opened her eyes slowly. Daylight. Her cheek was resting on plastic, cool and sticky. She saw chrome and more plastic. Black vinyl. She was uncomfortable. Finally she sat up, focussed properly, and looked around. It was morning. They were back in the car, parked as they had left it, in a side-street beside the College. David was asleep behind the wheel. Behind them was Michael Aarons, who stretched and yawned, and Charlie, still asleep. They were exactly as when they had arrived. Had they fallen asleep? Had she dreamt the whole thing? As she watched David, his eyes opened, and met hers. He grinned sleepily. Then he too looked puzzled. She saw memory flowing back, and the same questions entering his mind as hers. At last –

'Did you see?' she said. 'Have I been dreaming?'

'That place? The wolf? Charlie?'

He nodded.

'Yes. That's right. And something else. Something dark.'

She shuddered, then smiled. 'But it was all right – it was beautiful – in the end.'

'Yes – I saw.'

Michael Aarons stirred. He too was awake. David turned to him.

'And you, Michael?'

'I also saw.'

For a while they sat in silence. Something moved at Aarons' feet, wriggled into view, and stretched.

'Splodger!'

Michael Aarons smiled. 'Splodger was there,' he said. 'All the time. Don't you remember? I told you she would be important to us!'

There was one anxiety. They could not wake Charlie. Peaceful and happy he looked, and his breathing was easy; but they could not wake him.

'Let's get him back to your house,' said David. 'If he's not awake by then, we'd better get a doctor.'

As they drove away, Elizabeth looked back, then cried out and plucked urgently at David's sleeve. He stopped the car, and turned, as did Michael Aarons. It was an amazing sight. From the centre of the college rose a cloud – a heavy pall which at first they took for smoke. Then they saw what it was. Dust – mounting slowly and billowing, monstrous, in the morning light. The archaeologist's fears had been realized. The excavations at Hadrian's Grave had collapsed.

Neither Elizabeth nor her companions noticed two young men who stood by the college gates, looked at each other in surprise for a few minutes, then set off eastwards.

At six o'clock on a Saturday morning, the streets of East London are quiet. It did not take long to get Charlie to the Vicarage, and onto a bed. They telephoned the doctor, then gathered round. Splodger licked his hand, but he did not stir. The doctor came within minutes, but it was too late. The fact was, merely human physique could not endure the encounter which Charlie had endured, and survive. Quietly and without fuss, Charlie Brown had died.

Chapter Twenty-Five

Reactions

The next meeting of the United Nations Scientific and Economic Liaison Committee was brief. Once again, the facts to be presented to the delegates were simple. At 11.37 UT on the night of 5 March, those monitoring the progress of Siding Star had seen it abruptly deepen in rednesss, then disappear. Explanation of this phenomenon appeared, at one level, simple. Whatever had been approaching our system was now withdrawing. Deciding precisely why this should have happened was another matter. Various hypotheses were advanced, none of them particularly convincing.

What seemed clear, however, was that the particular danger to our planet had vanished. The diplomats had been right to do nothing. Noting this, they turned their attention to other things.

On Monday, David Adam returned to work.

In the darkness of Hadrian's Cave, he had faced his own crisis. Perhaps by the very starkness of contrast, that meeting with evil had recalled for him another moment on All Hallows' Eve – a haunting, challenging moment of joy that had accompanied his discovery of the wolf. The subsequent redemption of the evil, and the price Charlie had paid, had served to confirm that memory. David was sure (surer than ever) that somewhere, ultimately, there was purity – of joy and even, in some sense, of despair. Had he not glimpsed them both? But he also saw that there was for the moment nothing in humanity that was not ambiguous, including himself. And his place, ambiguities and all, was where he was. He was not conceited enough to imagine that he was brilliant at his work, but he was realistic enough to be aware that he was good. And he had (he suspected) a measure of integrity, a measure of decency, which were precisely the human qualities the job really needed. So, he must stay.

The decision came, in some ways, as an anticlimax. Yet once it was made, it felt right. And in the instant of making it, there occurred to him certain further courses of action that could be taken in the midst of those very ambiguities that had so troubled him. They might, of course, prove costly. But that, apparently, was part of the bargain. Elizabeth, with whom he shared all this, concurred. Within a few days of returning to Salisbury, he had acted – not without trepidation, but at least with some harmony of spirit. It remained to be seen how things would turn out.

Jacquie Austin sat at her mother's ancient bureau and gazed out of the window into Water Street. In front of her lay a note:

> Dear Princess,
>
> There is something here that I have to do. I fear it may mean the end of us. Forgive me.
>
> You have made my life gloriously happy.
>
> Think of me sometimes, Princess. But not too often. Be happy.
>
> I adore you.
>
> Charlie.

Beside it, a letter from Michael Aarons.

Finally, she fetched pen and paper, and began to write.

Dear Charlie,

Today I received from you the saddest and most beautiful letter I have ever read.

I went up to the University Library to be alone, for I was feeling very tearful, and not at all sure that if I had to talk to anyone I should be able to behave like a princess!

Later, when I had cried a little, I came back and met some friends and found myself talking and smiling with them as if nothing was wrong. Then I drove to St. James' Church, and sat there. It was quiet. For once, there wasn't even anybody cleaning!

I'd somehow known it would be. So I sat and became calm. Now I have come back to Water Street.

Charlie Brown, I have loved you. That's a fact. And nothing can alter it. I have loved you. Weeks ago (centuries it seems) when we first met, I remember writing in my diary, 'Today Charlie called me princess.' You didn't just call me princess. You made me feel like one. Thank you.

Jacquie.

She sealed the letter in an envelope, wrote his name on it, and then went out. She walked slowly to the East Battery, and stood there for a moment, where they had stood on his last evening. Then she leant over the rail, and threw the letter into the grey waters of the Atlantic.

For one instant, she felt that he was present: warm and reassuring. Then he was gone.

'Goodbye, Charlie Brown,' she said, and started to walk back. For a while she walked slowly – then: 'Come on, Jacquie Austin,' she said to herself, 'you pride yourself on being bouncy. So bounce!' She quickened her pace.

Sir Charles Dancy signed the last of his letters, replaced the top of his fountain pen, sat back in his chair, and gazed contentedly round his lofty, rather ugly office.

Granted the unpredictability of all human affairs, things actually appeared to be rather well under control. His Minister was safely packed off on a tour of environmental agencies in Canada and the United States, where it seemed unlikely that even he could do very much damage. The Siding Star business had, thank heavens, fizzled out, just when it had begun to look as if they would not be able to cope with the secrecy much longer. For the rest, there were, so far as he could see, no new crises looming, and the Department was a model of scarcely believable calm.

He picked up his telephone, and in a few moments had his call.

'Look, George, I'm going to take a few days off. The Department will know where I am, of course, in case anything unexpected crops up. But there's nothing brewing that I know of, so it seems a good moment.'

Something from the other end.

'Really? Oh, good. Well – they'll just have to explain it as they like, I suppose.'

Something else from the other end. Sir Charles laughed.

'Splendid! Then I'll plan to be back on Monday week, and to see you for lunch as usual. The club.'

Something further.

'Well done! I'll see you then. Goodbye.'

Sir Charles put down the telphone, and gazed benevolently about him. Softly but accurately he whistled a few bars from the first movement of the fourth Brandenberg Concerto. Emily and Robert were free – he'd already established that. It would be fun to spend a few days with them and the children. He stopped whistling, and slowly an ironic smile spread over his features. Why, he might even suggest they take a run up to Scotland.

Michael Aarons was seated at his desk, speaking on the telephone to David Adam in Salisbury. It was the first time they had talked to each other since the weekend, and both were still feeling its effects. Conversation was inevitably somewhat stilted.

Aarons was glad to learn that Elizabeth and Sproglet, despite their experiences, seemed in reasonable spririts. The two men talked for a while of Siding Star and Charlie Brown. Then –

'Incidentally, I owe you an apology,' said the priest.

'Oh? Why?'

'You asked for time to talk,' replied Aarons, 'and amid all that happened, we never did. I'm sorry.'

'Well – thank you for saying it,' said David, 'though it certainly wasn't your fault. There was just too much happening. The fact is – I think I've managed to sort out my problem for myself.'

'That's good,' said the priest.

'Yes,' said David, 'I really think it is. The thing was, I was having trouble about work. Thinking of giving up, to be frank. But I think I've sorted it out.'

'I'm delighted,' said Michael Aarons and meant it.

'So am I,' said David.

Several things had happened, some of them better than he could have hoped. He had written a memorandum to his superiors raising the whole question of the appropriate rôle of police in industrial action – well aware that his superiors might not like it. Somewhat to his surprise, he had found it endorsed by his Superintendent, who had written a letter in support. In a further burst of energy, he had instigated a second series of enquiries into the alleged rape – and, rather to his own amazement, these had actually produced a witness – a neighbour who could, in certain key respects, substantiate the victim's story. Naturally, this considerably altered the chances of an action.

'Yes,' he said. 'Some time, when you've about eight hours to spare, I'll tell you about it.'

Michael Aarons smiled.

'Good,' he said. 'I'll hold you to that.'

Chapter Twenty-Six

The End of the Affair

A few weeks later, Jacquie Austin came to London. She visited Charlie's mother, and his colleagues in the University. She also arranged to call at St Andrew's Vicarage, for she was determined to know something of the priest who had played so large a part in the last hours of her lover's life.

So, on a sunny morning in mid-April, Jacquie Austin and Michael Aarons met.

Naturally, she wanted to hear at first hand what had happened, and Charlie's part in it. Michael Aarons told her as best he could. She, for her part, felt a quick sense of trust in the priest, and found herself telling him much: of her love, and of her grief; of the letter she had written, and even of the sense of Charlie's presence that day on the East Battery.

Michael Aarons nodded.

'Yes,' he said, 'I think you are right to take that seriously. I have known of other lovers who had such a consolation. I believe the manifestation was real. And to give you hope.'

He paused, then –

'May I venture another opinion about what happened?'

She nodded.

'It is this. For Charlie not to have done this thing would be for him to have made himself less than he was. If he had made himself less than he was – he would have ceased to be the man you loved. He might have returned to you whole in body, but he would have been flawed at heart. And you might indeed have married, yet finally rued the day you met. Do you understand?'

'Yes,' she said quietly, 'I do.'

'As it is,' he said, 'you have something very precious. The memory of relationship largely free of treachery or disobedience. That is not to be scorned.' She was looking thoughtful. 'Forgive me,' he said. 'I have said too much.'

She looked at him. 'No,' she said. 'You haven't said too much. What you say is true. And after all – once a princess, always a princess.'

'Right,' said Michael Aarons. 'Don't you ever forget it.'

EPILOGUE

Splodger sat in the long grass by her favourite tree, enjoying the sun. For some time, she had watched with benevolent curiosity as a beetle climbed a stalk. Then, abruptly, she looked up and gazed across the fields. Her eyes were shining. But precisely what held her attention was not apparent.